HOT WATER

HOT WATER

A Novel

Kathryn Jordan

BERKLEY BOOKS, NEW YORK

THE BERKLEY PUBLISHING GROUP
Published by the Penguin Group
Penguin Group (USA) Inc.
375 Hudson Street, New York, New York 10014, USA
Penguin Group (Canada), 90 Eglinton Avenue East, Suite 700, Toronto, Ontario M4P 2Y3, Canada (a division of Pearson Penguin Canada Inc.)
Penguin Books Ltd., 80 Strand, London WC2R 0RL, England
Penguin Group Ireland, 25 St. Stephen's Green, Dublin 2, Ireland (a division of Penguin Books Ltd.)
Penguin Group (Australia), 250 Camberwell Road, Camberwell, Victoria 3124, Australia (a division of Pearson Australia Group Pty. Ltd.)
Penguin Books India Pvt. Ltd., 11 Community Centre, Panchsheel Park, New Delhi—110 017, India
Penguin Group (NZ), Cnr. Airborne and Rosedale Roads, Albany, Auckland 1310, New Zealand (a division of Pearson New Zealand Ltd.)
Penguin Books (South Africa) (Pty.) Ltd., 24 Sturdee Avenue, Rosebank, Johannesburg 2196, South Africa

Penguin Books Ltd., Registered Offices: 80 Strand, London WC2R 0RL, England

This book is an original publication of The Berkley Publishing Group.

This is a work of fiction. Names, characters, places, and incidents either are the product of the author's imagination or are used fictitiously, and any resemblance to actual persons, living or dead, business establishments, events, or locales is entirely coincidental. The publisher does not have any control over and does not assume any responsibility for author or third-party websites or their content.

PRINTING HISTORY
Berkley trade paperback edition / January 2006

Berkley trade paperback ISBN: 0-425-20757-9

This book has been catalogued with the Library of Congress

PRINTED IN THE UNITED STATES OF AMERICA

10 9 8 7 6 5 4 3 2 1

"Women are like tea bags. They don't know how strong they are until they get into hot water."

— Eleanor Roosevelt

HOT WATER

One

That was the place! All this way, and she'd driven right past it. She hit the brake, too hard. The car skidded sideways as she fought the wheel, adrenaline blurring everything. Next there'd be that life-before-your-eyes moment. Hold on. Don't flip! For a fraction of a second she thought she felt the right wheels actually leave the pavement. Then the balance shifted, and the spin lost its momentum. The seat belt bit into her shoulder as the car jerked to a stop.

She sat looking up through the spindly branches of some kind of desert tree, mesquite maybe. Heart pounding, breathing again. Jesus! Going too fast, easy in this car, not used to the way it responded. A few more feet she'd have had to call the dealership in Beverly Hills, tell them she'd run off the road into a tree, change the lease to purchase. No hiding that from Ralph. She could just hear him. "California! What the fuck are you doing in California? What happened to your sister's in Oskaloosa?"

She smiled. Well, she'd never driven a sports car before, or any vehicle that cost as much as a house, unless you could count Ralph's eighteen-wheel diesel Mack. She'd driven that, a few feet, anyway, back when it was new, before he built the business into a fleet of land moving equipment, Bobcats and belly dumps and graders, snow plows for winter. How could anyone get excited about a belly dump? But that was when things were different, when Ralph would take the time.

She opened her door, leaned out. The rear tires were still on the pavement. Good. She'd come this far, dreamed it for years, saved and planned, covered all her tracks, even the credit card bills, thanks to her sister. "You're on a mission," Lucille had said, laughing that crazy laugh of hers. "Hell, I'll go halves if you promise to tell me everything!"

She edged the car onto the road, made a U. Hidden Springs Spa and Resort, just as it looked on the Web site, only it seemed smaller in all this expanse. She'd never been in a desert before, never been west of the Mississippi unless you counted shopping in Minneapolis or visiting Lucille.

No wonder she'd almost missed it. Nestled below a cactus-studded outcropping on one side and a thick gray-green wall of tamarisk trees on the other, the entrance revealed nothing of what she knew was inside. She turned up the drive, gravel crunching beneath the tires. Perfect. Nothing glitzy, not one of the huge luxury hotels east of Palm Springs, not even a golf course. People came here for the water, the quiet, the secrecy.

Adults only.

Chills again. Ever since she'd walked onto the plane late last night she'd felt them. She'd be sipping her coffee, opening her peanuts, and there'd be a sudden surge, like hitting a pocket of turbulence, only the flight had been completely smooth. She touched the skin just below her throat, could feel the pulsing, her face hot. It was happening, and this time it was real, not just a fantasy. How many years had she been living on fantasy?

Ahead was a small gatehouse. Built of rounded stones, gathered, she supposed, out of the desert washes that fingered their way down from the foothills. In front was a stone fountain, beds of petunias and snapdragons. The "gate" itself was a steel bar, like at a railroad crossing.

As she pulled up, a woman in jeans and a polo shirt with the Hidden Springs logo came out holding a clipboard. Short red hair, no makeup. Fit, the look of a woman who's kept herself up, as if however many years she was over forty made no difference. Imagine.

Driving down from L.A. in this car, she'd gotten all kinds of looks, but the woman's eyes hardly flickered. Probably used to exotic cars here. The place was known as a getaway for the rich and famous, movie stars, Hollywood trysts since the '30s. She might see someone.

The woman leaned, smiling in the open window. Like Susan Sarandon in that baseball movie, except her hair was shorter and redder. Silly, the famous people would be guests, not employees.

"Good morning," the woman said. "Looks like you chose a gorgeous weekend. Cool for June. Your reservation is under . . . ?"

"Julia . . . Julia Reeves," she said. It was the name of her high school French teacher. What the heck. Julia. She liked the sound of it. She'd admired old Miss Reeves (not old, she realized now), so independent, lived alone, traveled to Paris every summer.

The woman scanned the clipboard. "Ah, here you are. Is this your first time, Ms. Reeves?"

"Yes, yes it is." First time, all right, her heart hammering again.

"Well, you'll love the stone cabin," the woman said. "Not really a cabin, of course. It's one of the original buildings, has some of our best antiques and stained glass. You'll see. It's just past the grotto, has its own little courtyard."

Tucking the clipboard under her arm, she handed Julia an open map. She wore no nail polish either. Nice hands. "You're here," she said, pointing. "Follow the road around to the office, there. I'll call ahead. Just let me get the license number."

She walked to the front of the car. How did one get such creamy skin? Julia wondered. Was it the mineral water? Or maybe a redhead thing.

When the woman came back, Julia noticed her eyes. Unusual shade of green, like new moss.

"Your first spa treatment is at one thirty, plenty of time to try one of the pools." She paused. "And . . . I see you have a guest coming later. Should I direct him to your room? I'll need his name . . ."

Oh, God. Do not blush! Name. She did not know his name. She'd only seen his picture. She'd have to call, tell him what to say.

"William," she said. Just popped into her head, out of her distant past, her only boyfriend before Ralph. "Yes, have William come to the room. He'll be here at six o'clock."

Just like that, and where did she get that voice? Nonchalant, as if she were famous, did this all the time. Must be the car.

You could be anybody in a red Lamborghini.

Two

Walking the cobbled path from the office to her "cabin," Julia was amazed. The photographs did not do it justice, but more than that—the entire atmosphere felt charged, as if the tiny lavender flowers on the bushes were breathing some elixir into the air.

Everything—trees, flowers, thick grass, the row of bungalows off to her right, even the path and her own sandaled feet—seemed outlined, crisp. The morning sun feathered through the huge tamarisks; she could see dust particles in the air, molecules swirling. When she lifted her hand, her

fingers were webbed with light. She could trace the veins, corpuscles filling, cells renewing.

She felt almost dizzy, and then . . . completely, miraculously calm. It was like looking out from a lifeboat and watching her past slowly, slowly upend, then slide, nice and easy, beneath the water. Twenty-some years. Gone.

The path turned down stone steps, and at the bottom she froze. It was what you'd imagine finding at the end of a long hike up a jungle trail. A clear pool shaded by palm trees and ferns and flowering vines, waterfall at one end, vapor rising where the hot mineral water tumbled over rocks into the pool. Its shape was irregular with rounded ledges, steps and niches that seemed carved from stone, all coated a pale blue, paler than the sky, the water's surface mottled with sunlight.

She wanted to untie the straps of her sundress and slip into the water in only her new lace thong. No, not yet. A half dozen guests were settled in various spots along the sides, leaned back on the blue walls, feet propped on Styrofoam floats, eyes closed, or sitting half-submerged on ledges, reading books. A couple was nestled near the waterfall, whispering, but the only sound was the soft tumbling of water. No one famous, at least no one she recognized.

She hurried on, the sun warm against her back. Silly thoughts, parallel universe, another dimension, beamed up,

her face on a milk carton. A mineral water stream meandered out from the grotto, passing not twenty feet from her
cabin, then murmured down a slope to her left, the path
crossing back and forth beside it. Flowers and grass, and
here and there another small pool edged with round stones,
all shaded by the thick tamarisks.

Strange tree, it grew in no particular form, branches curv-
ing at odd angles, some parallel to the ground, as wide as a
bench. You could sleep there, cradled. Like old grandfathers.
Standing at the top of the slope, she had the sense that the
whole compound was held in the arms of these fifty-foot
trees, the limbs, the ground beneath, everything cushioned
with their needles.

Kneeling by the stream, she let the water run over her
fingers, and although she knew, it still came as a surprise,
that it was hot. A thousand lakes and streams in Minnesota
and every single one icy cold, even in August.

She had died, that's it. The car had flipped, cut her neatly
in half, and she was dead. Here! Lovely thought. It made her
smile, made her want to dance!

Then, as she turned and stepped onto the little stone
bridge, she saw the young man from the office waiting by
the cabin door. He was holding her suitcase, a stack of thick
towels and a spa robe beside him on the wrought iron table.
In the office they'd joked about her "Minnesota-white" skin,

and he'd shown her on the map the secluded tanning decks. "Clothing optional," he'd said, as casual as his glance. Right, she'd thought, not a lot of tanning in Oskaloosa.

But now . . . the way he was standing there, sketched in the same crackling light. So California, Brad Pitt in shorts and tank top. And the way he was watching her . . . Oh, my! Hardly older than her son. She met his eyes. She did not care. Some gifts were just too luxurious.

"I took the long way," she said, smiling. "What a dream this place is." His shoulders, little prickles of sweat at the base of his throat. She imagined her lips there. "I hope I didn't keep you waiting . . ."

"No, no problem," he said. His fingers brushed hers as he took the key, tiny filaments tracing the air between, and a scent she couldn't place. Myrrh, desert sage?

"I'd be glad to show you more," he said. "Did you see the lake, the Zen garden?"

"No." She fanned herself with the map. "But first I must get wet . . . I mean, that grotto . . ." She pulled away from his eyes to glance over her shoulder. Wet. Did she really say that?

He laughed, "Absolutely." He turned, opened the door, stood back for her to enter.

Three

Julia lay naked on the high bed, listening to his footsteps on the path. She could still feel him, the insides of her thighs shivering. She moved her hands up her belly, breathed in, studied the water lily design in the stained glass skylight above, amber and blue-green, white blossoms. They did not make stained glass like this anymore. Nor furniture, dark and heavy with scrolled feet, cut-glass knobs.

His tongue on her nipples. The smooth, hard flesh of his back . . .

That it happened or didn't made not the slightest difference. Nothing is but thinking makes it so. And, oh, how skilled she was at living in her thoughts. Books. Fantasies. Enough to finally make one real. She reached and dialed the antique phone on the night stand, left a message for "William."

Odd, that her mind would call up the William from years ago. High school sweetheart. William Cathcart. He was on the debate team his senior year, smart and intense, a little frightening to her at sixteen, took her to the county fair, gave her Arpege. Then he went off on a scholarship to Penn State, and that was that. Probably a judge or a senator now. Would she have wanted such a life? Different constrictions, that's all.

The clock on the stone mantel said 11:10. Impossible. It was at least nine thirty when she'd left Beverly Hills. Was this place a kind of time warp, moments expanded into hours, days? She smiled. A lifetime in forty-eight hours. Unless the clock was just off.

She turned toward the mirrored wall closest to the bed, surveyed her reflection. "Minnesota white," indeed. But toned, anyway, thanks to eighteen months of almost daily workouts. She stretched on the sheets, touched her breasts. They were smaller now. She liked that. It was probably a sin to be so pleased with her body.

"Sin." She laughed out loud at the thought. A tiny embryo of a sin compared to the rest, a gateway sin, a marijuana sin. Crazy. Sunday school teacher rounds the bend.

Yet lately the whole concept of sin seemed a presumption. Reducing the immensity of God. How could we ever know? What if there was no sin, none except our labeling it? Projecting fear. Slipping from the path of who we were intended to be. She studied the colors in the stained glass. And where was the pattern for sin? In all of nature she could think of no evil outside the human mind. Her hands meandered farther, the knoll of her ribcage, flat belly, then stopped.

Not yet.

She stood, opened her suitcase and pulled on her new wisp of a bathing suit. She let her hair fall forward, tied the strap, then stepped closer to the mirror. She splayed her fingers over her abdomen, then down, tracing the little hollows on either side, the smooth bare skin of her very first bikini wax. Was it just yesterday? She'd come home, locked the bathroom door and trimmed the rest until it was only a ribbon of light brown fuzz in the middle. All but naked, pretty pink folds. Three gray hairs she'd plucked.

She turned her back to the mirror, looked over her shoulder, appraising. Not bad. It'd taken days of shopping to find a perfect narrow cut that didn't edge up her butt. None of that awful tugging. Of course, she'd had to buy two bathing suits, a six for her top, an eight for her bottom. One hundred eighty-six dollars for little scraps of nylon-spandex!

She imagined a row of doctors and lawyers nodding somberly as Ralph signed the commitment papers.

She faced the mirror again, grinning, hands on her hips. Wonder Woman! She had gone where few dare to go, she had faced the basilisk, fought the Gorgon, braved the gauntlet of dressing room mirrors. Laughing at her silliness, she stuck her thumbs in the elastic of her bikini bottom, let it snap. And, my God, leopard skin!

"Woman your age, look at you! What the hell are you thinking?"

The voice was so sharp and familiar she jumped. Her eyes shot up, and in the mirror for the briefest moment she saw her face mutate, wincing, cowering, and then . . . it could not be! Ralph was there, looking over her right shoulder, all red and puffy and angry the way he got. She blinked. No. Even if he had found out, he could never get here so soon. What was happening?

Her stomach tightened. She wanted to cover herself, but Ralph was standing between her and the towel. Stay firm, breathe. "Woman your age." Damn right, she would say. Forty-six, is there some law?

But something was wrong with him. He was fuzzy around the edges and wavering, as if he needed his tracking adjusted, a hologram losing its juice. And then, with a faint sound like bubble wrap popping, he dissolved.

Four

A slight shiver, like walking through a ghost, like someone breathing on the back of your neck. She sat on the bed staring at the space where Ralph had been. Shaking, eyes burning, afraid to blink, he might appear again. The B movie, just when you think it's all over, the creature pops back for a last scream.

She hugged her arms tight. Christ, now she was seeing things. Damn him! Trying to take this from her too. Like that time when she was eight months pregnant with Elizabeth. Her cheeks flushed, remembering. They'd gone out to a club with the couple next door, Charlotte and Bill something. Music rocking, oldies, who could resist? It was her birthday, he humored her. And she forgot her big belly under that silly froth of a dress, like a schooner with sensible shoes, and she tossed her head back and danced, eyes closed, until she felt Ralph's stare.

He was standing still, arms crossed, a stone statue in the middle of the dance floor. "You're making a damned fool of yourself," he said, loud, over the music and gripped her arm, led her back to their table, heat spreading up her chest and neck as if it might ignite the organza; immolated right there, like one of those wives in India. People trying not to look, ghost faces flashing in the pulsing lights.

She shrugged it off, of course, smiled to save the evening. Fatherhood had its own complexities, she supposed. They would adjust.

She was twenty-two then.

But it wasn't Ralph, she knew. Not now. It was her own guilt. Like medieval indulgences, paying in advance for her sin. She sighed. Sin again. With its zombie laugh, dirt clods and decayed skin, refusing to stay buried. Not that easy, honey, is it? The creature mocked. Think you can erase a few thousand years of conditioning just like that? Eve, Pandora, Mary Magdalene. Clever strategy, huh? These men. Call something its opposite, people climb right on board. Little war and conquest now and then to sweeten the pot.

She lay back on the bed, trembling. Maybe she couldn't go through with this, after all. This place, where time all but stood still, where the air seemed to whisper things it might be better not to know. Maybe she should just give it up, abort the "mission," go home.

Her eyes stung with sudden tears. No, no tears. She placed her fingertips on either side of her nose, pressed the socket bones, breathed in. Oh, she knew how to fight tears. She was an expert, a kung fu master at tear fighting. If she cried, she might not stop, and restoring a ravaged face wasn't such a snap anymore. Well, no red puffiness tonight, at least not her face. Her hands went to her mouth, too late to stop her mischief.

"William." She remembered his photograph on the Internet, dark hair, those amazing cheekbones, intimations in his eyes. She'd kept his picture on the screen just long enough to choose and click, the TV blathering through the wall. But then, she couldn't stand it, she went back, had to see him again. She smiled, how that sounded. She saved "William" in her RECIPES folder. "Oyster soufflé."

Once, soon after the kids were gone, she actually made that dish for dinner, with a nice salad, sliced cucumber and pear on a bed of endive, mandarin orange for color. And Ralph got up and walked out, as she knew he would. Ice fishing, said he'd get a steak somewhere. Just like that, the house all to herself, a quiet evening with a good book and Strauss.

Yes, she was bad, deliciously bad. And if she had to pay for her "sins" in advance with an occasional Ralph sighting, so be it. She glanced at the clock. 11:16. Of course, Hidden Springs time. In less than seven hours "William" would be here in person. She felt a billowing in her chest, like that crazy bungee ride at the county fair, the first bounce, oh, my God, then that tiny instant hovering at the top, the cord stretched to the very limit, just before the plummet.

Julia stood, swept her hair up, fastened it with a wide clip, slipped on her sandals. She started to wrap and tuck the towel over her bikini, then just carried it. "Woman your age." Damn right! She had already paid. Paid for William too, and she seriously doubted there could be a refund for that.

Right now, she would just get wet.

Tonight, "William."

Five

He stood at the foot of Mrs. Carlton's bed trying to remember why this had seemed such an all-fired great gig. For the first six months or so, anyway. He was being even more quiet than usual, and she hadn't heard him yet. She was in her pose, lying on her stomach, head turned away, the top of her feathery white negligee showing above the sheet, her perfect frosted-to-hide-the-gray hairdo unmussed on the pillow, and, of course, the satin sleep mask. Right out of a 1930s glamour flick, he thought, the room too, all mauve and pale green, nouveau art deco, she called it. Carpet so thick he had to brush out his footprints as he left.

Great gig. Lately he could hardly imagine why he'd taken the job at all, couldn't even seem to get started anymore without this little ritual of dredging up reasons. Okay, for one thing, Nancy Carlton was a regular, every Saturday morning, nine a.m. sharp, while Mr. Carlton, *the* Herbert J. Carlton, retired head honcho of something or other, was out teeing off.

Easy money. Yes, that's it. Mrs. Carlton's weekly envelope had covered his two student loans and half the rent. But the loans were long since paid, and he had enough saved . . . Enough. What was ever enough? He'd been thinking of buying one of those new luxury condos up in the cove, maybe lease a Lexus. Fit the image. And anyway, the routine here was simple, he never even broke a sweat, and when it was finished, he had the whole rest of the day free.

He glanced over. The envelope was there on the night stand, as usual. Ten crisp hundred-dollar bills.

Damn, he wanted a smoke, and he hadn't even fucked her yet.

"Is someone there?" Nancy Carlton said. Her frightened housewife voice. "Who are you? What do you want?" She lifted her head from the pillow slightly, as if listening, but she didn't turn over or take off the sleep mask.

His cue. He unbuckled his belt, slid it out, let it drop, mostly for the sound. He'd had to drive all the way to

Coachella to find a belt with one of these huge Chalino buckles that'd make a thud even on this carpet.

"*No te muevas,*" he said softly. "*Si te mueves o gritas yo tendré que hacerte daño.*"

She'd wanted it in Spanish, of course. If you move or scream I'll have to hurt you. He didn't even speak Spanish. That first week, he'd almost gone and asked Grandma Estella. Christ! She'd have taken an iron skillet to him, or worse, started praying. Probably both.

He almost smiled, then got control. Grim, menacing. "*No te mueves . . .*" He unzipped his jeans, didn't take them off. Mrs. Carlton liked the feel of the zipper biting her thighs. He knelt on the bed, repeated the magic phrase. "*Si te mueves o gritas . . .*" Even now he wasn't sure he had it exactly right, but what the hell, it made her wet.

"Who are you?" she whispered. "What are you doing? Oh, my God! Please, no!"

He threw off the sheet, flipped her onto her back, lifted her gown. The rough stuff was getting easier. Nancy Carlton and her pathetic charade. "*Acuerdate,*" he said. "*No hables o gritas. ¿Verdad, que no quieres que te haga daño?*" It startled him. He'd never made it sound so real.

She put her hand to her mouth, shook her head, whimpering.

Her whole damn life was pathetic, a travesty. Rich bitch,

trapped behind gates. Portly husband out in his cart, clueless. Or maybe not.

But when he pulled out his dick, he knew he was in trouble. Shit. Couldn't even slip on a condom like this. He took it from his pocket, already out of the wrapper. Clients hated this reality. After the initial flash of his health card, he tried to keep the process as unobtrusive as possible. Preparation and dexterity is what it took, and practice. At least Mrs. Carlton never watched.

He had maybe ten seconds to get hard. Pussy. Think pussy. Right there staring at him. Concentrate. He closed his eyes, thought of Linda, his old girlfriend, his ace in the hole. She'd gotten him through more than one of these . . . occupational hazards. Linda taking him in her mouth like he was the world's last Popsicle, her eyes grinning up at him, loving it. How long since he'd had a blow job? Never at work, that's sure.

He looked at Mrs. Carlton lying there, starting to wonder, probably. Concentrate. Linda with her long legs wrapping around him. Linda straddling his face. He remembered her scent, gave himself a few strokes. There. Maybe. He managed the condom, then pushed in, felt himself get harder. Not rock hard, but . . .

"Oh, my God. Oh, my God! Oh, yes, do it! Like that. Fuck me! Fuck me!"

He lifted her hips, was getting his rhythm now, pounding

the way she liked, when there was a scratching and whining at the door. At first he thought she might be too far into it to notice, but the whining grew louder, then yelping. Damn dog!

"Mitsy? Is that Mitsy? Why isn't she in here?" She stopped thrusting, put her hand on his chest, and he felt himself wither. She pulled off the sleep mask. It was a shock seeing her eyes. He could not remember when he'd last seen her eyes. Blue and cold as gem stones.

"Javier, what in heaven's name were you thinking?" A completely different voice, the way she talked to the maid, each word wrapped neatly . . . in barbed wire. He slid out of her. She pushed him away, scrambled off the bed, a flurry of white negligee hurrying to the door.

"You know how Mitsy likes to be here. I can't believe you didn't let her in. You did it on purpose, didn't you?"

It was true. He'd thought it might be nice. Just once without those little black buggy eyes watching from the other pillow. He could swear the little bitch liked to watch, her tongue drooling on the satin. Lupita must've opened the door, let Mitsy into the hallway. He stood, fastened his pants, retrieved his belt. Fuck it.

Mrs. Carlton came to him, the pug in her arms, excited by the reprieve, licking her face. "Oh, poor baby," she cooed. "My poor, poor baby. Left outside all alone." She held up the dog, its pink tongue hanging. "There, see, Javier is sorry. Aren't you, Javie? Give Javie a kiss to make up, sweetie . . ."

Then she noticed his crotch, all zipped up and put away, belt through the first loop. Her eyes hardened. "What are you doing? I'm not finished. You can't go yet."

He just looked at her. He had an almost irresistible urge to land the heavy buckle squarely on the stupid dog's head, then wrap the leather strap around Mrs. Carlton's throat until her eyes bugged the same . . .

He let the belt drop, a souvenir, turned, ignoring her tantrum. What could she do, tell her husband? He walked out. In the living room, Lupita's eyes widened at the stream of curses coming down the hallway, glass shattering, then the maid smiled, said something in Spanish he didn't understand. Didn't need to. He used the front door. Fuck the service entrance.

In his Tacoma, he fumbled out a cigarette, pushed in the lighter, then dropped it, of course, had to fish the damned thing from under the seat. Not a good day.

He took a long, sweet drag, checked his cell phone. The Minnesota lady. William. She wanted him to be William. What the hell was that about? Six o'clock. Hidden Springs Spa and Resort. Great place. And prepaid, the first night, anyway. Up to him to get a second.

Or maybe he just wouldn't show.

Six

This water was like none she had ever felt. Blood warm, silky. Not a single guest was in the grotto pool now, and the blue coating shone even paler in the late morning sun.

On the bottom step, Julia bent her knees and sank to her chin, savoring. A dozen minerals, yet clear and odorless as an Alpine lake, not a whiff of sulfur. Unique in all the world, the brochure said, an underground lake seeping its magic ions up through an earthquake fault, water so hot it had to be cooled first, 148 degrees!

Fingers splayed, she swept her arms in wide arcs through

the water, a mermaid gathering sea blossoms. She could feel the minerals, whole battalions infusing her open palms, health commandos in silver suits and full gear swimming upstream, hosing down blood cells, polishing platelets, out with the bad, in with the good.

Deeper in the middle, she bobbed on tiptoes, reached a small Styrofoam float, slid it under her chest, stretched out her legs. Reptilian, she imagined, nostrils just above the surface, lounging, belly full. The pool wasn't more than twenty feet across. She drifted slowly, slowly . . . hardly a ripple. Paleozoic, lush, continents mostly water, primordial swamps untainted by humans.

With webbed fins she swam/crawled onto the widest ledge, turned back toward the center, perfect for basking. She hooked her clawed toes in a crevice in the rock wall and lay full length, resting on the float, only her nose and eyes out of the water, alert for the slightest movement. Okay, maybe evolve a little, ease into it, eon by eon, but never ever give up that feral core, that propensity for swallowing meat whole. She smiled, licked her lips, still submerged. The water did have a slight taste.

She would bring William here tonight, taste him with it.

Seven

Eyes closed, Julia listened to the waterfall a few feet away, the murmur of bearded palm trees, fronds brushing each other in the slight breeze. Now and then a snippet of birdsong, insect hum, cicadas. Or were they called locusts out here? No wonder the air felt so alive; it was alive, that constant murmur, magnified now by the water. She could feel it in her chest, like entering a high voltage area. Anticipation.

An odd clacking sound came from the bushes behind her, repeating. An animal, probably, but one she'd never heard before. She stayed perfectly still, waiting, muscles coiled.

How lovely it was to belong to a species in which the female is every bit as powerful as the male. Or as ferocious, anyway.

The waterfall suddenly went from a trickle to a gush, tumbling over the rocks. Automatic, the evolved part of her brain supposed, triggered when the water level subsided. The constant flow from the pool out into the stream made filters and chlorine unnecessary. Only in times past would they think of something so simple, natural. The influx of new water sent heat spreading under her legs, up her leathery middle. Oh, my. Pity it wasn't yet mating season. Soon, though.

Languid now, she curled her thick tail and drowsed, an epoch or two. Voices. She stirred, opened her eyes, suddenly quite hungry. Guests were slipping quietly into the pool, observing the PLEASE WHISPER signs almost hidden in the tropical foliage. She resisted an instinct to slither off her shelf, grab a leg, do her famous death spin.

The water was fogging her eyes some. She blinked, watched two hazy young women settle onto a ledge across near the steps. They held paperback books carefully above the water, talking intently, giggling, and *shh*-ing themselves when they forgot to whisper. They looked like models, tall and tan and beautiful. A bit lean, but delicious. Except for the implants.

A middle-aged man with glasses and thinning hair got in. More meat than the other two put together. He found a spot, began reading what looked like a manuscript or screen-play. The famous Hidden Springs casting couch, his "date" probably in having a spa treatment. Who could he be? She hadn't considered the possibility of seeing a renowned di-rector. Not Spielberg or Lucas. Certainly not Woody Allen. Who else would she recognize?

More voices. She moved only her eyes. Coming down the second set of steps where the pool curved around were an older lady and gentleman, in their late sixties, maybe a little older. People of a certain strata could keep themselves up. Amazing, she thought, how you can spot people with money even when they're wearing hardly any clothes. The way they carry themselves, a certain air, as if ringed by invisible atten-dants. She squinted. Heavens! That was Gregory Peck!

She sat up quickly, the Styrofoam float shooting out across the pool, and everyone glanced over. She blushed. One of the greatest film icons of all time and she's doing her prehistoric croc imitation. Must be the water.

But it could not be Gregory Peck. Gregory Peck was older, in his late eighties . . . No, Gregory Peck was dead. Just last year. She closed her eyes, then looked again. They were in the pool now. Uncanny, you'd swear it was him, but perhaps, yes, this man was a bit thinner in the face. The lady had noticed her staring. Mustn't be rude. Julia scooted off the ledge, retrieved her float, paddled over.

"I didn't mean to be impolite," Julia whispered, "but for a minute . . . I thought you were Gregory Peck." She smiled to the lady, then back. "I mean, I forgot he had . . . passed away. I'm from Minnesota. We rarely see celebrities there, you know. Well, the governor . . . before."

He looked at her a moment, then laughed, a little too loud, didn't seem to care. "No harm, no harm at all," he said. "You're certainly not the first. Actually, I was Mr. Peck's double in *The Boys From Brazil*."

"Really!"

"Mm hmm."

My God, the voice, the way he cocked his head back when he laughed, the twinkle. It was flawless. What, had the man studied Mr. Peck so well he'd absorbed every mannerism?

The silence seemed to swell then, as if she'd enticed him into using up his Hidden Springs word ration. The lady, his wife, Julia assumed, was smiling pleasantly enough, but she also hadn't missed the leopard print bikini.

"Well, it's nice to meet you," Julia whispered. She added a you-two-have-a-nice-stay smile and paddled on. Amazing. *Boys From Brazil*. To her right the pool narrowed in a kind of corridor, shaded by rock walls. Pots on niches with leafy philodendrons, and from crevices an occasional bromeliad, ferns, orchids, purple and pink and white, swaying on thin stems.

She came to a low levee with steps up and over. On the other side was a shallow pool, hotter, she presumed, although there were no jets. As she stood, the breeze felt only a shade cooler on her skin, air and water the same temperature.

She could almost feel the couple looking at her, marveling, perhaps, how such a small swatch of material could stay in place on her behind. For a moment, mingled in the trickling of the waterfall, distortion of sound on water, she thought she heard, "Nice ass," in that deep voice, and a woman's laugh, but no . . . don't be silly.

She stepped over, lowered herself in. Oh, my, yes! Hotter. Good. The hotter the better.

Eight

The light was different here. There were more gaps in the palm branches above, turning the smaller, shallow pool an even paler blue, almost white in the noon sun.

Julia found another float, propped her feet on it, balanced the other under her neck, then lay back, ears submerged, eyes closed, weightless. The only sounds were far away, muffled echoes as in a submarine. Let the water do its work. She concentrated on the flickers of light patterning her eyelids. Soft rose, dusty yellow.

It had started with the colors, she'd have to say now. One

ho knows? Might have been right after the infa-
oyster soufflé, but she remembered a different quiet in
the house, Ralph already down at the yard. He no longer
trusted a foreman to oversee the dispatching. Or maybe
Ralph just preferred the noise and bustle of the yard, men
shooting the breeze as they clocked in, all those lovely trucks
idling. Away from the house, anyway, from the silence that
hung between them now that the kids were raised and gone.
Her silence.

Then, when she walked into the bathroom, those colors!
Like fingernails on a chalkboard, the colors suddenly that
wrong. Sickeningly wrong, metal-spoon-on-a-broken tooth
wrong. Burgundy and hunter green, gold faucets, gold towel
racks, gold flecked tile, and that cutesy wallpaper trim
around the ceiling. Pheasants! Sitting on the toilet, she
could hardly make herself pee with these colors. Why now?
she had wondered. Like going around for years with dark
glasses, then suddenly removing them.

A pedestal sink and chrome fixtures, that's what she'd
have, white floor and walls, oyster white, Greek island white,
everything spare and clean. She could use a project. She
threw on jeans and a T-shirt, but even as she went downstairs
and through to Ralph's office, she saw it was too late. The
color pestilence had spread through the whole house. The

living room like the lounge in a gentlemen's club, all hounds-
tooth and leather, an elk head staring from over the fireplace, Ralph's stupid bear claw ashtrays. Well, the bathroom
would do for now. She spent a lot of time there anyway.

She rummaged in Ralph's desk drawer, found the Home
Depot card, would not stop to call and ask permission. Not
one more day with those goddamned pheasants! But the
drawer caught on something, wouldn't close.

She reached back, pried out a fat envelope. Law Offices of
Franklin, Jones and Patterson. She unfolded the papers. Grant
Deed. Property. You didn't get a deed for a truck or a loader.
She scanned the legal language. East half, section fifteen . . .
Record of Survey . . . Lake of the Woods. Why would anyone
want forty acres on Muskeg Bay? She thumbed through the
next pages. A hunting lodge, of course. Good, was her first
thought, a place for his trophies, she *would* redo the living
room. Of course, she would have to sign. She scanned again.
No, these were the final papers, all stamped and notarized.
January 2003, over a year ago. Her name was not there. Not
on the contract. Not on the deed. Not anywhere. Only Ralph's.

He hadn't even told her.

She slumped back, almost laughed. What a picture
crossed her mind; someone walking in and finding only an
indentation here on the leather chair.

When? she wondered. When, exactly, had she disappeared?

The breeze shifted, brightening the patterns on her lids, and when she opened her eyes, she was looking straight into the sun. The branches moved again, shading her. She waited out the momentary blindness, sun circles, and then she noticed, amazing! Tiny fairy lights flitting on the underside of the palm fronds. Like Tinkerbell. At first, she could not figure the source, and then . . . it was the water reflecting sunbeams back up to the branches. She lay enveloped in silence, suspended in the dance, the play of light and water and air, like watching music, a secret choreography.

A different movement caught her eye then, higher, to the right. And when she saw Ralph sitting forty feet up on the tamarisk branch, she was hardly surprised. The only curious thing, when she focused more precisely, was that this was not the Ralph of today, the Ralph she'd left in St. Paul. This was a younger Ralph, a high school Ralph, long armed and lanky. And he was grinning at her. He seemed poised, as if about to do one of those ninja flips, branch to branch, land here in the water and ravish her.

Oh, she remembered that grin, although she hadn't

thought of it in years. The time he took her snow goose hunting in North Dakota, seventeen, their first . . .

"Julia."

The voice repeated twice before she heard it through the water. Christ, her hallucinations were talking now. How could Ralph know the name she'd chosen, her Hidden Springs name?

But the voice wasn't coming from the tree. Much closer.

"Julia. Ms. Reeves . . ."

She sat up. The young man from the office was standing on the edge of the pool, holding a towel for her. She hadn't even noticed the low steps on that side, the path behind him leading out through the bushes.

Impossible to look at him without picturing his tongue in her mouth, his hands lifting her. She blushed.

"It's twelve forty-five," he said, smiling. "On the form, you selected lunch by the lake, remember? And your treatment is at one-thirty, so . . . Of course, nothing's set in stone here. We can always rearrange . . ."

"No," she said, "I am hungry. Not to mention turning into a prune." She held up wrinkled fingers to show him, like a little kid. Then she stood, waded across, the air chill on her heated skin. She turned her back to him, and he draped the towel over her shoulders.

"Nice suit," he whispered, close. She could smell the sun on his skin. "I was counting your spots just now," he added, "but I kept losing track."

She laughed. Flirting. Nothing in all the world made you feel so alive. She met his eyes. "Well," she said, "if you want to try again, I promise not to move, not a muscle." She used that certain tone, drew the words out, left spaces for him to fill.

"Oh," he said, "I wouldn't want that. Never tell a woman not to move . . . At least not when her crab salad is waiting." He put his hand on her back, started her toward the path.

At the turn, she glanced up over her shoulder. Ralph was gone, the tamarisk branch swaying slightly.

Nine

They must teach this in masseuse school, Julia thought. Modesty Training 101. Lying here completely naked while the girl rubbed on a thin layer of clay, one leg, then the other, shoulders, arms, chest, carefully tucking and retucking the sheet so your essential parts are always covered. A skill as amazing as the touch of her hands, young and strong. Pretty girl, in shorts and a halter top, her own skin beautifully bronzed, honey blond hair in a thick braid. Her name was Heather.

Julia wanted to tell her, never mind the sheet, I don't care. Modesty was for her other life, not here. If she had her way, she'd spend the rest of her days naked, her body scraped and slathered and kneaded regularly, in a cabana like this, palm-frond roof, walls covered with papyrus reeds, a paddle blade fan sweeping from side to side, meditation music in the background.

Cleopatra, she was, covered head to toe in the famous Hidden Springs' natural green mineral mud, dug fresh at sunrise. Egyptian Clay Body Wrap, they called it.

"There," Heather said softly, "all done. Now if you'll roll this way just a little . . ." Like the old tablecloth trick, blink of an eye, and the sheet was gone, turned into a thin blanket, patted tight around her. A mummy. "We'll let the minerals work awhile," Heather said, "then I'll come back, shower you off for your massage."

Julia nodded from her cocoon, eyes closed under little pats of sea algae, consciousness drifting, scent of ocean breeze, water sounds, slow *shhsh* of the fan . . .

She did not remember showering, but she was back on the table, lying on her stomach, no blanket, no sheet, naked. Two sets of hands now, anointing her with sacred oils, one massaging her calves and feet, the other her shoulders.

Oh, sweet Jesus!

She did not have to look. It was Heather and the lady from the gatehouse, the one with the moss-green eyes. As if synchronized, they worked her, thumbs and knuckles pushing out the last bit of tension, rotating the balls of her feet, kneading her neck, her scalp, and gradually she noticed the alternating pressure, deep tissue, and then softer, exquisitely soft. Ostrich plumes tracing circles on her lower back, then the soft skin just below her buttocks.

This was not in the brochure. Sometimes, well, we have a way of knowing when a guest wants . . . more. The hidden part of Hidden Springs.

Did she hear that, or just sense it? Intoxicated, her mind hazed with the musk of patchouli, bergamot. Thoughts whispering. Relax. This is all there is. Nothing else matters.

The hands nudged, and she turned onto her back, did not open her eyes, afraid they'd disappear. Fingertips circling her nipples, lightly, then down her belly, the insides of her thighs, bending her knees just a little. Touching her as only another woman knew how.

So it was true, what she'd heard? Could it be her truth?

The hands stopped then, and the sensations actually intensified, her skin cells arching up, like baby birds clamoring, feed me, feed me! She wanted to cry out, bring them back. More! Yet it intrigued her, how the sudden absence of touch could be so powerful, an ache starting above each thigh, like fuses burning upward, another down her abdomen . . . Please. If she were captured by an enemy, she'd tell them anything, sell her mother, her children. Just start again.

They did, before she could speak it out loud. And again. Touch then absence of touch, deeper each time. Priestesses unfolding ancient secrets, mysteries that lay always just beyond man's grasp. Kabbalah, the Grail, *moksha*, the Tao, quantum physics, fusion. And just how many angels can dance on . . . this little nub? Center of the universe!

The curtain drew back, wooden beads clicking together, then footsteps.

"How are we doing?" Heather said, removing the pats of sea algae from Julia's eyes.

She tried to find words, could not. "Mmm." Nothing like a coat of mud to hide a blush.

Heather laughed, a sweet laugh, unencumbered, joyous. The laugh of someone who's twenty-two or -three, Julia thought, with the vast majority of her mistakes still unmade. The laugh of someone who goes to work each day in paradise.

Heather unwrapped the blanket, handed Julia a towel, helped her off the table, legs a bit unsteady.

Julia looked at her hands, her body. What fun being green!

Kermit. Swamp creature awakening fully evolved, ready to get it right this time. Although she kind of missed her plated armor.

"Follow me," Heather said, "the shower *palapa* is across the lawn."

Ten

She woke later without the slightest idea where she was. She'd been dreaming of crooked houses with water pouring in, floors so slanted you had to crawl your way to the door, whole rooms falling off into the sea. She'd been standing on the rim of a jagged hole over a thousand-foot drop. What did it mean to dream of houses that wouldn't stay put? She waited for the images to fade.

But when she opened her eyes her first thought was, how nice that Ralph had added a stained glass skylight and stone fireplace.

Then she smiled, remembering, bit by bit, her day. No

wonder she'd slept like the dead. After her "treatment," she'd sunned awhile on the "clothing optional" tanning deck, swam in the saltwater pool, cavorting like an otter, soaked again in the grotto.

A squeal rose now in her chest; so this is how it would feel, reading off numbers on a million dollar lottery ticket as you come to the final match. Yes! She was still here, still Julia, it wasn't over.

Over . . . my God, it was just beginning. William!

The clock on the mantel said 5:46. Fourteen minutes to get ready! Heart racing, she scrambled off the bed, gathered her makeup case, blow-dryer and curling iron from her bag. In the bathroom, she poured a glob of foundation into her palm, was about to dab it on, when she noticed the difference in the mirror, her skin rosy from Egyptian clay and California sun, healthy. Pity to start clogging pores again. But go without makeup?

Then she realized with a sudden, delicious calm, this was not a date. She had paid. And if William thought her . . . less than beautiful, it did not matter, not one whit. An amazing concept, like someone slapping sense into you.

She stared at her reflection, trying to absorb what it meant. Such freedom, power. Simply facing the world with your own face, like a man. Not having to paint or primp or cater. She could hardly put words to the feeling. Like being rescued, a giant crane lifting off huge slabs of history for survivors to wriggle out into the light.

She washed the foundation from her palm. Mascara, just a touch. No time to start over with her hair. She brushed it out, shaped it around her face. Even her hair felt healthier; the perfect cut to leave straight. Who would've thought she could wear it like this? She'd been perming her hair since the late 70s.

In the other room, she slipped on a cotton sundress, light yellow to accent her new tan, or wannabe tan. The dress had a bodice top with eyelet trim, ribbon straps tied at her shoulders. It fit even better than when she'd bought it.

No underwear.

No last look in the mirror either. It did not matter. This was her fantasy. She had paid. She hurried out to the little walled patio and sat at the wrought-iron table so she could see him walking along the path toward her.

Eleven

"William," he said at the gatehouse.

The lady smiled, then pulled her eyes away to check her clipboard. He was used to that look, the slight intake of air. Crazy, but he was starting to think this effect he had on women might be more a curse than a gift.

"Pretty cool for June, isn't it?" he said casually. Talking weather helped put them at ease.

"Oh, yes, lovely," she said. Fluttering, she opened a map, showed him the parking area and the path to the stone cabin.

No need to tell her he had been here before.

"Well, William," she said, "you enjoy your . . . evening."

"Thanks." He drove through. On another day he would've added, "You have beautiful eyes, you know." He could rarely resist the way a woman blossomed with just a small compliment, that little burst of surprise, then delight, sudden shyness to cover it. They were all beautiful in that moment.

Well, no free compliments today. He was still pissed from this morning with Mrs. Carlton. Given half a chance, too many of them became Mrs. Carlton. But the real pisser was that he didn't pick up the envelope on his way out, severance pay. Never mind. He didn't need it, although most of his business was in the winter months, November to March, snowbirds. By August he'd have to dip into his savings. A weekend with the Minnesota lady would help. He had decided it would be unethical not to show tonight. She had already paid. Unethical. There was a joke, considering his line of work. He had told himself it was temporary. Pile up a savings, then go to grad school. Too late for this year.

He parked between a Mercedes and a red sports model he couldn't quite place. What a car! He got out, looked at the front. A Lamborghini. Lamborghini Murcielago. He'd only seen pictures in magazines. He walked around it twice, careful not to touch anything, probably had an alarm from hell. V-12, 6 speed, all-wheel drive, horsepower must be pushing six hundred. If it weren't for the alarm he'd try the door, just to sit behind the wheel. Man!

He gave a last look, then walked past the office and down the stone path. On the turn before the little bridge, he stopped abruptly. Could that be her? He checked the map. Yes, that was the cabin.

She was nothing like he'd expected. Younger, at least from here. Hardly looked much older than he, five years, eight at most. No way could she be over forty, and with the sun shining behind her . . . she could be walking out of a wheat field. Minnesota.

She saw him and seemed to register his looks without so much as a flicker. He crossed the bridge. She stood, smoothed her dress. Pretty dress. Pretty face, completely natural. What a change that was. Not the usual stretched and tucked look from multiple lifts, no Botox or permanent makeup. Like trying to beat the mortician to his job.

And the rest of the package . . . Not bad. Not bad at all. He'd been with a lot of women in the last three years, more than he cared to count, but one thing he'd decided early on was that Madison Avenue didn't know shit about real beauty.

"Lucille?" he said, stepping onto the patio, and she laughed, happy, as if this were the perfect way to start.

"No," she said, "Julia. Lucille's my sister. I used her

credit card." She offered her hand, as if they'd just been introduced at a reception.

"You're taller in person," she said, and then thought, shit, how stupid is that? As if you could tell height from a photo. She started again. "I . . . I hope you didn't mind the William thing. I didn't know your name, but . . . you don't look at all like a William."

God, he was gorgeous, like Johnny Depp in that Don Juan movie, only more Hispanic, skin like Antonio Banderas. Jeans and a white collarless shirt, those dark, dark eyes . . . She felt sick. Something horrible was going to happen, nuclear attack, earthquake; she'd come to California just in time for the Big One. A person just did not have this much luck, not in a lifetime, much less a weekend. Stop. Stay calm, don't let it show. Her nickel.

"William's fine," he said, smiling, "not a problem." No need for his real name, unless she asked. He doubted she would. So she was married, why else borrow a credit card? Too bad. Married women were more often sad and bitter, or just pathetic like Mrs. Carlton.

"Shall we sit here for a few minutes?" He held the chair for her, took the one across. This part was always awkward, better to get right to it. Nothing like a good fuck to break the ice, but he could tell she wasn't ready. Besides, he was curious. Why would a woman who seemed about as worldly as a patchwork quilt, who could walk into any bar and get laid in twenty minutes . . . why fly all the way across the country and pay for it? But he knew better than to ask. Asking broke the spell. The first rule, never talk about your real lives. Still, they couldn't just sit here.

"So, what did you have in mind, Julia?"

She looked away. "Oh, I don't know." The words came with a snap. All her silly fantasies, all her "she had paid" toughness, and now that he was right here . . . She wanted to go inside, fix herself better. Maybe the whole thing was a mistake. Maybe she couldn't do this.

She turned back, softened her tone. "Or, I . . . I thought we might go for a drive."

"A drive?" He pictured the cab of his Tacoma, cluttered with Taco Bell wrappers, ashtray overflowing. Not to mention his "goodie case" disguised as a laptop. Smart to leave it in the truck. This woman hardly seemed the type for black leather and purple dildos. Never mind vibrating butt plugs.

Then she said, "Well, it's just, I rented a Lamborghini. Incredible car. Seems a shame not to drive it." A lease purchase, but no need to go into that. When she returned it on Monday the deal would cancel, except the weekend charged to Lucille's credit card.

His eyes widened a little, but he said nothing. He had years of practice not overreacting to a lady's wealth. She didn't seem that rich. Rented, she'd said, but still.

"Oh, we wouldn't go far," she went on, "just a little drive, and then . . . Then we could come back and have dinner. The restaurant here is wonderful. There's a balcony that looks out at the mountains. We could watch the sunset."

There, he thought, there was beauty. A look to slay dragons for, if there were any dragons left to slay.

"I checked the menu," she went on, "they have this special Hidden Springs gazpacho to start, and rack of lamb and a braised salmon and a whole tray of desserts, raspberry swirl cheesecake and baked Alaska, and . . ."

He knew then precisely what she needed.

He stood, lifted her to her feet, kissed her, his hand behind her neck, softly at first, holding her as she gasped, tears starting, which he kissed away, until gradually, gradually she began to let go of whatever had held her, and she kissed him back, hard, greedy, starved kisses, there in the sunlight.

And what amazed him most was that he was willing to trade, okay, postpone, a drive in a Lamborghini Murcielago to give her what she needed.

Twelve

He lifted her in his arms, carried her inside, set her on the bed, kissing her mouth, her neck, shoulders, untying the ribbons. He undid the corset top, grateful that he'd mastered the one handed hook-and-eye technique. Her breasts, beautiful . . . She moaned, tugged at his shirt, and he slipped it off. She stared at his chest, pulled him to her.

He knew he should slow down, she had traveled all this way, paid in advance for the whole evening, and yet he wanted to devour her, now. Hard, probing kisses. His hand slid under her skirt, searching for panties, but there were none, her skin warm, already moist. Only a ribbon of soft hair and the smoothness of newly shaved flesh, those sweet hollows. Maybe she wasn't as unworldly as he'd thought. Shit, slow down. What was he thinking, touching her there already?

Julia felt the brush of his fingers and gasped, kissing him, clutching his back tight, as if only that would keep him from vanishing. He was real, not one of her crazy fantasies. This was happening. She arched her hips.

He stifled a moan. Fuck, he never made noise. But that sudden ache below his balls, how long since he'd felt that? So much for the master craftsman with his careful rules. It was his trademark. Half his business was from referrals. For new clients the code was absolute: Assess. Individualize. Deliver. Okay, he got that from his last education course, Lesson Planning for the Secondary Level, but it applied. Helped him focus, anyway. Focus. Yes.

Slowing his hand, he whispered against her throat. "Tell me, Julia, tell me what you want."

It took several moments for his words to register through the sensations. Then her eyes shot open.

"No!" she said, scooting away. "No, I will not tell you what I want. I'm sick of telling and telling, and . . . damn it, you're supposed to know! That's why I wanted a . . ." Her voice wavered. Professional. Why not say the word? It seemed one thing to go through with it, another to speak it out loud. Did men feel this? This . . . shame, having to pay for what should be a gift?

"Damn, fuck, shit!" she said then, covering her eyes. "I won't cry. I swear . . . oh, hell!"

He did not smile at her spew of profanity. "*Shh*, come here, Julia. Come here." He reached, brought her back, held her. Christ, he'd almost blown it. Should've seen. "I'm sorry," he said. "I made a mistake. I do know what to do. Just relax, relax." He wiped her eyes, touched her cheek.

Moments passed, and suddenly he couldn't help it, he laughed.

"What?" She sniffed, looked up at him. Making fun of her now? So there was the catch. She'd prefer a man a little less handsome and more kind.

He'd been thinking of all the countless asshole stories he'd heard from clients. But this guy, her husband . . . He hadn't thought they made assholes that big. But he wouldn't say that.

"If you want to know, Julia," he said, "I wasn't working just now."

She searched his eyes . . . and then he saw her bullshit detector click in. Every woman had one, some better than others. But it wasn't bullshit, not exactly.

"Piffle," she said. "And I want you to work. That's why I'm here."

"Piffle?" He laughed again. He'd been waiting for her to say something in Minnesotan. "Well, if you're gonna talk dirty . . ." He sat up, pulled on his shirt, tucked it in, started re-hooking her bodice. It was a lot easier to unhook than hook.

"What are you doing? Don't . . ." She stopped his hands.

"It's okay. I'm starting over. I'll go out and come back in. Trust me. You'll like it."

"I will?" She took a moment to consider.

Then he stood, and her eyes went directly to his crotch, not a small part of the effect he had on women, if he did say so himself. When fully inspired. The ache had not subsided.

"Oh, my," she said.

She was up on her knees instantly, pulling her dress over her head, laughing, playful now, almost brazen. And he saw that she was one of those rare women who look good in clothes, but even better naked. A lot of guys were tit men, but to him anything more than a B cup was ponderous. For him, it was all about mid section, landscape and proportion, the slope of rib cage to belly, knoll and valley, the precise arc of waist to hips. And Julia had it. One of his favorite places to kiss was that little glen of flesh there just below the hip bone.

The guy was more than an asshole, he thought, a fool, an idiot! Although he understood men like that, in a way. A woman can seem so mysterious, daunting, if you never learn to pay attention. And with these meat-and-potato men, if the slightest hint of inadequacy gets through the armor, their only defense is to shut down.

She moved to the edge of the bed, still on her knees.

"You can start over later," she said, reaching for his belt. "And I'll tell you what I want, William. I want it all. I want to learn. I want you to show me everything, your whole repertoire. But for now," she said, "I just want this."

Unzipping him, her eyes widening. "Oh, yes, this!"

Thirteen

When he pulled the condom from his jeans pocket, he fumbled. What? He never fumbled! But when he glanced at Julia still on her knees, she was grinning.

"Here, let me," she said, taking him in her hands. "Oh my gosh, it hardly fits. Goodness!" She tugged at his jeans, and he kicked them off.

As he entered her, she cried out, put her hand to her mouth, and then thought, why? The cabin shared no walls, and if someone was out on the path, who cared? It wasn't pain, no, although she sensed . . . oh, my . . . there could be an edge so exquisite between pleasure and pain as to blur the difference entirely. With each thrust she had to concentrate not to let her eyes roll back in their sockets.

She wanted it all, to watch him watching her, his eyes holding her, as if gauging the slightest tremor, and she wanted to watch his body moving, savor his shoulders and chest and belly and . . . oh, my God! . . . at the same time to close her eyes and just feel . . . Lord, sweet Lord Jesus! This could not be. She could feel herself starting to come. Impossible. She hadn't even set her mind to start to try. Hadn't even begun to think up a scenario. This was the scenario . . .

"What are you doing?" she said, opening her eyes. He had stopped, was barely moving.

"Making it last," he said, "slow down, Julia. Slow down."

Making it last! She'd always had to work just to make it happen. She hadn't had an orgasm during sex since 1988. Her thirtieth birthday, she remembered exactly. A weekend at Moose Lake without the kids. Since then, her strategy was to start on her own, a half hour or so before Ralph came to bed, and still most of the time she had to finish in the bathroom . . . with the damn pheasants. Unless he fell asleep in front of the TV.

Oh, she read the articles in women's magazines with all their silly statistics. Seventy percent of women have only clitoral orgasm, perfectly normal. Well, she didn't care. It was not the same. She wanted penetration. Like this. She put her hands on William's ass, pulled him deeper, arching to him. Oh, God! But he just held there, not thrusting.

Although, that slight pivoting was nice.

"Take it easy," he whispered, touching her cheek, kissing her lips, her eyes. Soft, soft kisses. "There's no hurry. We have all night. I'm not going anywhere."

She looked into his eyes, listening to the lull of his voice. What else could she do? He would not move, not even pivoting now. Only his voice, rocking her gently.

"There," he said, "let it go, for now. If you let it go, it'll come back stronger. Trust me. I know these things."

That smile. She couldn't help but smile back, and then she breathed deeply, and again, long intakes of air, then release. She felt her body relax, as if her very cells were pulling in oxygen, expanding. Her cheeks and neck still burning.

Okay, William thought, the break was as much for him. Truth was, he'd been about to lose it. If she kept moving like that, her hands gripping his ass, he wouldn't make it 'til 6:30 much less the whole night. Rule number two in the code; never come until the job is complete. Like that year he worked construction before he got his BA. Job ain't complete 'til the inspector signs it off. Job, yes, job, he had to remember that. He wanted another night with her. No, he wanted the money. Yes, money, concentrate. Keep it about money. Get her to stay through Monday and he wouldn't have to draw from his savings until September.

He began again, slow strokes. It was her moans, throwing him off and how warm and tight she was around him. Work. Think of something else. Oil needed changing in his Tacoma. He'd take care of that tomorrow. Maybe clean his aquarium. The refrigerator. It'd been a couple months since he'd cleaned the refrigerator. There, he was past it.

He speeded up just a little, deep thrusts, nice even rhythm. He could feel the soft cushion of her cervix. Once in a long while there'd be a woman whose cervix was like another button, more nerve endings, he guessed. Like . . . what was her name, Helen something . . . Wainwright. Helen Wainwright never came without deep penetration. His first client. A gem of a woman. Julia might be like that. The way she was arching . . . She wanted it all, she'd said, his whole "repertoire." Well, a weekend wasn't enough time. A sampler platter would have to do.

Man, the way she was moving on him, those noises. He doubted he could slow her down again. Of course, he could come now and still get it up later, but in his . . . professional opinion . . . man, she was good . . . it wasn't quite the same, like an athlete, you lost . . . a certain edge. Stick to the code.

Man! It was not going to be easy. The muscles in his abdomen straining, his balls tight . . . starting again. He lifted her hips, sat back on his knees, taking her with him, didn't miss a beat.

She opened her eyes, moaning, "No, please," pulled him back down.

She wanted his weight on her, the rocking, almost bucking now. But just that slight change of position had been enough. He got control. She was close. He leaned and whispered magic in her ear, his incantations of lust.

Her eyes widened, rolled back, the moans became huge gasps, yelps, as her nails dug into his shoulders. "Oh, God! Oh, God!" He felt her insides spasm, tightening around him, had to fight for control. But he kept thrusting until she collapsed, panting, eyes closed, hand to her throat.

He pulled out quickly, lay beside her, gathered her against his chest and held her as she sobbed. This was his signature move, his tour de force. He always felt like an acrobat in a circus now, the stunt incomplete without the perfect bow. He smiled. Crying was one of the truest marks of success.

In minutes she drew away, lay on her back. He left her alone. Yes, stick to the code. He would've drifted off to sleep otherwise. He wanted a cigarette, but he knew not to get up and go outside, not this first time. In her haze she might not notice, but still . . . Women took longer to wind down, needed the closeness. Such a miracle, the female body, with its infinite capacity for pleasure. What he always felt watching this was awe. No wonder men had to find ways to diminish them.

In another minute he checked her. At first he thought she was asleep, lying so still, but her eyes were open, staring up at the skylight, grinning.

"You okay?" he said.

Okay, Julia thought. She understood now. First, you had to accept that it's all illusion. Then just take the step, make your own reality, and grab what's left. After all, were these moments any more a "sin" than living twenty-some years in a box? She did not think so. Although, what were the odds it would be like this?

"Julia? Are you okay?" William raised on one elbow.

Her grin widened, still staring at the skylight. "I hardly think okay is the word." She spoke slowly as if waking from a long sleep. "I've been lying here trying to think of words . . . besides thank you . . . and there aren't any. There just aren't. But . . ."

Her voice did a kind of reality shift. "The sun is starting to set." She nodded toward the stained glass, the lily pads a darker shade of green. Then she turned to him.

She looked even younger, her cheeks flushed, and her eyes . . . The glow. How he loved the glow.

"William," she said, "I was thinking, is it all right if we do the drive tomorrow? I'm starved. Aren't you? You must be."

She touched his cheek, tender, caring, as if he had just walked into the kitchen, set his lunch pail on the counter after a twelve hour day.

"Let's go," she said, "let's go have dinner."

Fourteen

They were still sipping their gazpacho, the sky a deepening pink-orange over the Santa Rosa mountains, when Julia asked the question.

"And how did you get started in this career, William?"

They almost always asked. He usually made something up, some tear-jerk story, his mother on dialysis awaiting a kidney transplant. But Julia was so ingenuous. There was an odd innocence about her, considering how good she was in bed. Career, she'd called it, hadn't even hesitated. He looked at her across their balcony table, that sky working its masterpiece in the background. He didn't think she would laugh.

Okay. "I . . . I wanted to be a professor," he said, watching her eyes. Nothing, not a flicker, "of philosophy."

"Philosophy." She nodded, went on buttering her roll.

He chuckled. What a joke, this guy who fucked women for money, but there it was, the truth. "I started as a history major," he said, "U.C. Riverside, about an hour's drive from here, but I had a scheduling conflict in my third year, and there was a course in medieval philosophy, Dr. Snider." He smiled, remembering when he'd first walked into Dr. Snider's class. "She's Indian, from New Delhi, married to the head of the department. Hardly five foot tall. Sometimes she'd wear a bright yellow or orange sari and sometimes a leather miniskirt. She liked to surprise us, I guess. With her lectures too. I was hooked. All those minds, the books . . ." He laughed. "I used to imagine myself as this silver-haired scholar, expounding on Maimonides, Thomas Aquinas . . ."

Julia had brought her glasses to read the menu, and now she looked at him over the rims. "Yes, I could see you as that. A very handsome professor."

Play along, she thought. Oh, he was good, a master. She could feel herself getting moist again. And he seemed so young to be able to sense the exact conversation to work as foreplay. Books had been her salvation. Besides the den, she'd taken over one wall in each of the kids' rooms for her floor-to-ceiling bookcases, catalogued like a library. Saved the lower shelves for the children. She wondered if William did this with all his clients, read them at a glance, create the perfect background story. Most men didn't have a clue that conversation was foreplay.

"Go on," she said, smiling.

"Well," he leaned back, "you know what a BA in philosophy is worth? Nada, zip." He lifted his Beaujolais, as if to clear the edge from his voice. "Anyway, I ran out of money. So I took some education courses, thought I'd try substitute teaching, maybe get on full time, emergency credential. Save for grad school." He looked down. "It was a nightmare. Especially high school, five overloaded classes, a couple hundred squirming teenagers, half of 'em with shaved heads. I couldn't do it."

Big mistake, he thought, sniveling like this, breaking the illusion. Stay the hero, Lancelot. Never, never show your real life. Shit, he'd let her eyes draw him in.

"I taught for a year after I got married," Julia said easily, "eighth grade." She had liked it all right, but hadn't really minded giving it up either, when Ralph insisted. "But substituting," she said, "that's a whole different thing. And there are no shaved heads in Minnesota. Too cold." She laughed, then turned suddenly, taking in the sky behind her.

"Oh," she said, "never in my life have I seen such a sunset! It's so big out here in the West, so open." She'd been starting to believe him, see him as a real person. Not sure she wanted to.

He'd been flattering himself, William thought. She wasn't interested in his life. She was on vacation. He was just part of the scenery. He stood, offered his chair. "You really should sit here, Julia. You can see it better."

"Oh, no," she said, turning back, "I'm fine, and look . . ." She held up her hands, scanning the air around them. "It's everywhere. See? Everything's all pink, almost shimmering. It's like we're inside it. Luminescent. I love that word. Luminescent." That's what she wanted, just to play and flirt, be a girl again, wrap herself in make-believe. Why not? It's what she'd come here for. If only there were somewhere to dance. How long since she had danced?

He sat again, watched her finish her gazpacho.

"Oh, this soup! And in a few minutes, William . . ." she raised an eyebrow, her voice lowered, husky, "it will be dark."

As if on cue, the waiter came and lit the candle lamp on the table, filled their wine glasses.

When he was gone, Julia leaned forward, whispered. "And I'll tell you a secret, William. This place. It isn't quite real. I'm not kidding. It's like another dimension. Probably the earthquake fault, fumes seeping up. But things happen here. Magic things." She smiled. "You'll see."

It was her voice, yes, some quality that made you want to

believe whatever, just to hear it. He imagined her telling stories to her children, if she had children. She must, although the idea brought the usual twinge. It was always hard to think of a client as a mother.

He sensed movement then and glanced up, did a double take. Gregory Peck was standing right there, his wife at his elbow.

"So we meet again," he said to Julia, that deep voice. "Beautiful evening, isn't it? How 'bout that sunset!"

"Ah, Mr. and Mrs. Peck. How nice." Julia smiled playfully. "This is William, my date."

William fumbled to his feet.

"I think I've seen you somewhere," he said, shaking William's hand, "on a set, maybe? You're in the industry?"

"Well, yes, Mr. P—" What was he saying? He'd done one scene when he was seventeen, a TV movie shot in the Indian Canyons. And Gregory Peck was dead.

The man laughed, "Wainwright. I was Peck's double in *The Boys from Brazil*, a long time ago. I'm Charles Wainwright," he nodded, "and this is my wife, Helen."

Fifteen

Helen Wainwright, his first client. William kept the surprise from registering on his face. He'd been so absorbed by the Gregory Peck resemblance, he hadn't noticed her. But it wasn't such a coincidence. Helen adored Hidden Springs, had brought him here several times, after that first night at the Marquis Hotel.

Helen smiled and took his hand with the aplomb one would expect of such a woman.

"William?" she said, the slightest twinkle in her eyes.

He nodded, his name for the weekend. Steady. Not the first time he'd been in this awkward position. Once at

Melvyn's in Palm Springs, he and his date, Barbara something, had sat a few tables over from Mr. and Mrs. Carlton.
He'd thought Nancy Carlton hadn't even noticed until she
grilled him the following Saturday morning, "How old is
that woman?"

"Actually, I'm not in the industry," William confessed
now, "I was just an extra once. Answered an ad in the paper."

"Well, you should be," Helen said. "You are definitely
leading man caliber." She held his eyes a moment before
turning to her husband. "Charles, give the young man your
card. Sometimes all it takes is that certain connection."

"Of course." Wainwright pulled a card from his wallet.

The waiter appeared. "Your table is ready, sir."

"Yes, well, you two have a good evening."

They watched the couple follow the waiter into the
restaurant.

William turned the card over in his hand.

"See," Julia whispered, "uncanny, isn't it? Even his voice."
She'd noticed how Mrs. Wainwright looked at William.
Clever, the bit with the business card. A way he could con-
tact her. Who could blame her?

"Yes, uncanny," William said. He sat, slid the card into his
shirt pocket. Uncanny, all right, he thought, considering the
fact that when Helen hired him, the doctors had just given
her six months to live. A returned breast cancer. That was

three years ago. Obviously she'd gone into remission. He had been number four on her list of things-to-do-before-I-die, her husband in full agreement, she'd said. He felt a splinter of guilt. It was one thing to agree to such a request, another to shake the guy's hand, take his business card . . .

The waiter brought their entrées, and William was grateful for the diversion, Julia portioning out shares of salmon and lamb. "So I won't bother you by taking bites off your plate," she said, "I know how men hate that."

"Not me," he said, but he was still thinking of Helen. Three years, and since then he'd seen the effects of half a dozen mastectomies. Women whose husbands couldn't get past it. Actually, he'd rarely seen the physical effects (the emotional far worse, of course). They kept themselves covered, except for one who became a regular for a while, Mrs. Kensington, Susan. They used to take showers together, and the hardest thing he'd ever done was avoid glancing at her scars. He'd made love to Susan, made love to her bravery. When she stopped calling, he knew.

"Are you all right, William?" Julia said. "You don't like the salmon? I'll give you back the lamb, if you want. Here."

"No, no." He took a bite. "It's great. I'm fine."

He studied Julia's eyes in the candlelight. No, he would not tell her about Helen. She seemed to have forgotten her question, anyway, how he got started in his "career." Sitting in a bar on Palm Canyon Drive, the Hair of the Dog, when Helen Wainwright had walked up with her proposition. Ten one-hundred-dollar bills, which he felt guilty taking, at first. Beautiful woman, even as gaunt as she was then, her head wrapped in a chic turban. It was an honor to be on her list of things to do before she died.

And he had already decided not to go back to substituting; no more babysitting. He'd frame houses right through the summer before he'd do that again.

He considered this "career" temporary. Just until he saved enough for a PhD. Might as well have the luxury of going full time. This was a study in itself, if you thought about it. Intriguing, trying to fathom what brought each client to him. A woman like Julia. He looked at her across the table, eyes closed, savoring each bite as if it were ambrosia. *Earthquake fault seeping fumes, magic.* No, he thought, remembering his morning fiasco, Nancy Carlton and her sleep mask. No, never a client quite like Julia.

Sixteen

A wide stone stairway curved down behind the restaurant and met the path to the lake, the mineral stream burbling along beside it. In the halo of garden lamps they could see mist rising from the hot water.

Julia let go of William's hand, crouched beside the rocks, dipped her fingers in the stream. "I can't get over this," she said. "Even when you know, there's still a surprise when you touch it, and it's hot. Amazing." She stared at the ripples her hands made. "It's like even the water is in disguise. Nothing is as it seems." She smiled. "What philosopher said that, Mr. Professor?"

He laughed. "Every one of them, I'd say. It's a first principle. The root of all study. If things were as they seem there'd be no need to figure it out. Although nihilists would probably break it down further, 'Nothing is.'"

He crouched beside her, dipped his hand. "Wow, it is hot."

"But you have to touch it to find out," she said. "It seems just an ordinary stream otherwise. So touching is the proof." She put her hand to his cheek. "That is, if we can believe our senses." She tried to remember which philosophers questioned empiricism. Aristotle? Descartes? It'd been years. She read mostly fiction now.

"Oh, I believe!" William said, laughing. He kissed her, then stood, helped her up.

They were walking off dinner and a four-inch-tall New York cheese cake with raspberry swirl and chocolate fleur-de-lis. They stepped over the stream, then past shadowy trees across the lawn. The lake was some sixty feet wide; on the other side it tumbled over rocks and down to a smaller pond.

They tossed bread-stick pieces to the small fish boiling the surface, and Julia wondered how they could survive, until she touched the water and found it cool. Twenty degrees warmer than any Minnesota lake, but still cool.

A series of larger ripples crossed the surface, and at the same time, from behind them, came that odd clacking sound she'd heard this morning in the grotto. She imagined being surrounded by strange miniature clacking crocs that hunted in packs. Then a bevy of turtles the size of dinner plates stretched their wrinkly necks at the lake's edge.

She tossed crumbs. "Here, you old panhandlers."

"Only they'll never be homeless," William said.

That clacking again. Julia turned. In the shadows was a spindly form, maybe two feet tall. It clacked louder, and she reached for William's arm, prickles on the back of her neck.

"What on earth?" She half expected some shrunken version of Ralph, a demented toddler like in that horror movie, *tsk tsking* her.

"A roadrunner," William said. The bird appeared from the shadows, lowered its head in a beeline across the grass, skinny cartoon legs a blur. Then it stopped a few feet away. It hunkered down, as if settling onto a nest, lowered its head, wings spread flat on the ground, hugging the earth in a kind of salaam.

"What's it doing?" she whispered.

"I don't know." He shrugged. "Roadrunners do weird things, but I've never seen one do that. They're predators. You don't want to be a lizard with one of these guys around. Maybe it's the moon." A rim of white blinked through the far trees.

"So are there coyotes here too?" She peered into the night.

"Maybe," William said, smiling. "Coyotes do come in from the hills sometimes. Or could be a lady roadrunner somewhere close. Might be his mating dance . . . Hey!" He looked down. A turtle was trying to make a snack of his shoe.

Julia knelt, placed crumbs in a line, and he lumbered over, blinking his turtle eyes, red and black painted on the sides of his head like a tired old warrior. Cool light edged across the lake as the moon topped the trees.

She glanced up at William, watching her. For a moment he seemed just someone she'd met, not hired. Just "hanging out," as her kids would say. A new clacking sounded from a tamarisk limb off to the right, and with a flurry the roadrunner was up, sprinting to the call.

William took her hand. "Come with me, Julia," he said. "There's something I want to show you."

Seventeen

William led her back up the path toward the stone cabin. Show me, she thought, yes, show me. His kiss, just his hand touching hers sent chills. But when they reached her cabin he led her on around the corner and along the walled patio. What was he doing? She hadn't even noticed there was more to the building, as if it had grown, doubled its size while they were at dinner. Would hardly surprise her here.

Separated from her half by a narrow corridor was another unit, built of the same rounded gray stones. Beside the door was a large stained glass window, palm tree and sand dunes, purple mountains in the background. A light was on inside. It felt awkward standing here by the door to someone else's room.

"You know the legend," William whispered behind her, "that Al Capone built this place as a hideout from the Feds?" She could feel his breath below her ear.

She smiled. "I thought that was just marketing."

"No one knows for sure." He kept his voice low. "But it adds up. The restaurant was a casino. The spa was where they kept the ladies." He raised an eyebrow. "All those tiny rooms, the only windows thick stained glass. And in the waiting area there's a wall safe as big as a refrigerator. Did you see it? All ornate. Who would need such a huge safe?"

"Marketing." She nodded, teasing.

"Okay. Wait, you'll see." He led her down the corridor, stone walls on both sides, a roof above, like a medieval castle.

It did seem strange that they would build the corridor outside.

He stopped at another smaller window, high on the wall but made of clear glass. "Here, I'll boost you," he said.

The curtained window cast a faint light, but the passageway beyond was completely dark. She resisted the impulse to peer into the blackness, felt his hands on her waist. As he lifted her she let out a small yelp, put her hand to her mouth.

"*Shh*, don't want to get caught snooping."

She found a footing in the stone, her heart beating faster. He held her, his chest bracing her hips. What if someone came around the corner, how would they explain? She pulled herself higher. Through a gap in the curtains she could see an old-fashioned parlor, plush red velvet sofas and chairs facing a large fireplace, tasseled brocade draperies, red and gold, a full-sized bar with pillars and scrollwork, mahogany or cherry wood. More stained glass and beveled mirrors. Like a 1930s brothel.

"It's the original furniture," William whispered. "There's a table with the initials A. C., and you can't see it from here but the bedroom mirror has a bullet hole in it."

"Right," she said, laughing down at him. "Like the gun turret on the roof. It's in the brochure. Marketing."

"I know." He boosted her higher. "But the photograph. Can you see the photograph?"

She scanned the room again, expecting a portrait of the craggy-faced mafioso, proving nothing.

Then she saw. Over the fireplace was an enlargement maybe four feet wide. Even from here she could tell it was a photograph, not a painting. She leaned closer, straining to see, nose to the glass. At first, it looked like only a panorama shot of empty desert, rising to the mountain pass she'd driven through this morning. Nothing but sand and rocks and sagebrush. Then, toward the bottom, she noticed tiny clumps of palm trees, only an inch or two tall in the photo, and, my God, it was the "cabin," this very building, the same stones she was touching now. And parked to one side by the low wall were two black gangster cars.

"Oh, my gosh." She looked again at the background which was at least nine-tenths of the photo. Where was Palm Springs? Nothing, not the slightest trace of a town, no windmill forest, no power poles, no freeway, not even a road, just this one solitary structure against the vast sweep of desert. 1930. A world vanished.

What better place for a hideout? She imagined those cars driving ten miles an hour along an unseen dirt road, trailing plumes of dust. Men in black pinstriped suits helping laughing women from the backseat, flapper dresses and cloche hats, flasks of bootleg whiskey.

She heard a sound inside and turned. Through a doorway she could see a sheeted mound moving on the bed. "Oops, someone's there!" She let go, William lifted her down and they hurried through the black corridor, hands skimming the rock walls. She imagined time whirring backwards, and they would walk into different lives. Not until they came out into the moonlight and she caught her breath did she tell William the unlikelihood of their being noticed.

"They were, well, occupied."

"You saw it?" he said. "Not the couple, the photograph."

She nodded, smiling. "Oh, yes. If not Al Capone, someone in the same business."

He laughed. How beautiful she was, eyes bright with adventure, but he couldn't bring himself to say it. Didn't want words to seem part of the package.

"Come on. There's one more thing." He led her around to the front of the cabin, then off the walkway. He parted some bushes and she stepped through. Close to the wall was a large wooden trapdoor.

"A storm cellar?" she said. "I didn't know they had storm cellars in California."

"They don't."

He looked around to see if anyone was watching, then pulled the door open, laid it back on its hinges. A shiver of cool air breathed out at them, the musk of damp earth.

"The suite has a second bedroom with a back door," he said. "We passed it in the corridor. Capone, or whoever, had it worked out, apparently. The Feds came to the front, he'd be out the back and around here. The way we just came."

He got out his lighter, flicked it and took a step down, held his hand to her. "It's an escape tunnel. Want to see?"

Eighteen

Julia hesitated. He looked like Odysseus beckoning her into the netherworld. She wasn't sure she could trust her mind for such a journey. If she had visions aboveground, what might she see below? She wanted to ask how he knew these things, but it didn't matter. She stepped forward, took his hand. She had lived her whole life without seeing, wasn't about to back away now.

Still, her legs trembled, and he steadied her down the stone steps. Only a small circle from his lighter flickered around them, the rest black. She thought of snakes and crawly things and hugged close to his side.

"Careful," he said, as they ducked under a beam. A tunnel just high enough to stand in, the walls and floor packed dirt, wood planks above, fingers of roots coming through here and there, cobwebs.

She saw this bit by bit as he moved his arm, casting pockets of light. Spaced along the walls were square support columns, like a mine shaft. They inched forward, the flame revealing only a few feet in front, shadows closing behind. The smell of earth stronger with every step. She imagined the underground river gurgling deep below their feet, thought of bending to touch the floor, see if it was warm, but no way would she give up William's arm. The air coming out of the black chilled her bare arms, and she shivered.

"How far does it go?" she whispered.

"I don't know. I've never done this before." For once those words were true. Helen had pointed out the tunnel, but they didn't go inside. "I was told it comes out on the other side of the hill."

"The hill! Beyond the entrance? That must be several hundred yards."

"I know. They say he kept a getaway car there. So he'd be long gone by the time they saw the dust."

Their hushed voices sounded hollow, like in a tomb. She thought of Juliet waking amid bones and rotting flesh.

She thought of earthquakes, walls caving in. She thought of spiders . . .

Stop. Breathe.

"Why the hell are we whispering?" She spoke loud, defiant, chasing the fear.

He looked at her eyes, laughed. And the lighter flickered out.

She cried out, thought her heart would stop, but then he pulled her to him with such force, found her lips, kissed her, there in the blackness. She stumbled back against the wall, and he pinned her, kissing her again and again, hand on her throat, filling her mouth with his tongue.

She closed her eyes, useless to try to see. Felt him hard against her, replacing the fear, no, embracing it, riding it. Exquisite terror. Dionysus, the Maenads, whirl head back, beat the drums. Stare down the beast. Heart pounding, racing. Alive. It was what she'd come for. Did he sense this too? Snakes and scorpions be damned! Take me. Oh, God, take me!

"Julia."

He had to have her, now. To hell with his policy. He found the ribbon straps, jerked them from her shoulders, kissing, tore open her bodice, hooks and eyes popping. Her breasts, the flush of her skin on his lips, her pulse, nipples hard, the scent of her, the taste. He could not stop.

He pulled her skirt up, undid his pants, reached into his pocket, sheathed himself. One handed; there was a feat. No fumbling now. He pushed in, easy, so wet. He held her leg in the crook of his arm, pushed deeper, hard, grinding, lifting her with each thrust, kissing, devouring, taking her lip in his teeth.

She clutched his shoulders, gasping, crying out, the wall scraping her back, dirt crumbling on her neck. She didn't care. Didn't care.

Nineteen

She could only brace against him, carried by his hunger. Feeding on her. She was the flesh offered up to the unknown, and at the same time, fed by it. That he could need her so. She wanted to see it in his face, the depth of it, this force that drove everything, grew crops, filled rivers, moved planets, but when she opened her eyes, she saw nothing. Not a pinpoint of light. Blind. Only sound and touch and taste.

In moments he made a wrenching cry and shudder like a soldier brought down in battle, and slumped against her. Dying, they called it in the Renaissance. "And when he dies cut him out in little stars and he will make the face of heaven so fine . . ." She wanted to cradle him softly, pet him, but she was still pinned against the wall, the taste of dirt on her lips. She waited.

"I'm sorry, Julia," he said in another moment, "really, I . . ."

"Don't."

When William could move, he fastened his pants, found his lighter in his pocket, not the slightest memory of putting it there, and they staggered up into the moonlight. He sheltered her while she fixed her skirt, pulled her bodice together, managed to clasp a few bent hooks. Then he swung the trap-door closed.

A quiet settled over them as they walked the few yards to her room. Inside, she dropped her dress to the floor, lay on the bed. He brought a towel and wiped the snail tracks from her thighs, the dirt from her neck and shoulders.

"There're other things I can do, Julia," he said, "if you want."

"No, I'm fine," she said, "really." An awkward moment passed, and then she said, "What time is it?"

"Nine fifteen."

She smiled. Of course. Hidden Springs time. The evening young, and there was still tomorrow.

"Well," she said, "I think . . . we should go get in the water. I'm a bit sticky. Did you bring a bathing suit?" It felt odd to talk of ordinary things, like returning from somewhere far off, exotic, to find nothing changed, everything changed.

"It's in my truck," he said, "I'll get it." He touched her cheek. "You sure you're all right, Julia?"

She closed her eyes. "Oh, yes. Yes."

He left the door unlatched so she wouldn't have to let him back in, started down the path. He'd make this up to her, bring his goodie case from the truck. They'd play. If she wanted. An option, that's all.

The other, he wouldn't try to figure out. It just happened. Not everything had to have a meaning. And he wasn't sorry. No man in his right mind would be sorry. First time he'd lost it on a job, though. What the hell. She was leaving after tomorrow anyway.

All right, Julia thought, smiling, stretching out on the bed, savoring the soreness, her back scraped from the dirt wall. Asking if she was all right. My God! She would take this night with her. It was hers, she owned it, like a jeweled necklace too priceless to ever wear.

You could get through years with such a night. A night to blot out laundry rooms and kitchen sinks, walls that needed painting. She could sit by Ralph for hours now and not even see the TV, not even need a book to take her away.

Decades would blink by. She'd be on her deathbed, wheezing out her last breaths, surrounded by kids, grandkids, and still she would have this night. The children would look at each other, puzzled. "What did grandma say?" "I don't know, it sounded like *William*."

Julia laughed out loud, got up, put on her leopard print bikini.

Twenty

"Carry me piggyback," Julia whispered when she could no longer touch bottom. She reached for William's shoulders, pulled herself up, and he paddled them across to the wide ledge. They lounged side by side, chin-deep, heads propped against the coated rocks, silent, soaking up minerals. Only the moonlight, hum of cicadas, waterfall tumbling at one end, a few other couples nestled in corners.

The grotto pool was glorious in daytime, Julia thought, but at night! Enveloped in darkness, disembodied; the glow off the water made everything below the surface disappear, warm and hushed. It felt sacred, like worship. A temple pool circled with foliage, the air a blend of blossoms and musky branches. The tamarisks like tall priests.

She thought of what had happened in the tunnel. Could there be a sanctity in that too? Practically strangers, and yet the anonymity seemed part of it. Like the wearing of masks, celebrating ancient rites, drums and chants, the slap of flesh on flesh, simply honoring the rawness. Male. Female. The yin and yang. The ancient Chinese believed man absorbed female power and essence through intercourse, the more the better. Hindu temples carved with sex positions. Even now somewhere in Japan there was a village festival where they paraded giant carved penises through the streets.

Julia felt her cheeks flush, William lying right here, their skin touching. Renegade thoughts, yet she'd read about pagan sex rites, and that's how this felt, the act transformed by ritual, a celebration completely unrelated to everyday life, and sacred. No ties, no expectations, no layers of resentment. No going through the motions.

She felt a smile start, let her body slip farther, the water covering her lips. Oh, such elaborate constructs to justify pleasure. Yet without "sin," there'd be no need to justify. How lovely, such a world. She gazed up through the branches at the night sky. She could sleep here, have breakfast brought in the morning.

"Did you see that? There." William sat up, pointing.

She saw only a swatch of white disappearing into a palm tree. She edged up. "What was it?"

"An owl," he said. "A white owl. A family of them lives in the trees across the parking lot. That's only the second one I've ever seen." He lowered his voice. "In Mexico the white owl means death, or anyway a bad omen. Here the Indians believe they're protectors. The species isn't usually found in the low desert. Except here."

"Really?"

He smiled. "Or that could be more marketing."

Marketing, Julia thought. She had a list of words now that would connect instantly in her mind. *Roadrunner, photograph, tunnel.* Like notches guiding the way back. Jelly beans.

Shadows moved toward the center of the pool, a man barely supporting a woman in his arms, the way you teach a child to float. Lean back, relax, you won't sink, I'm here, I've got you. Gliding her slowly, around and around, her hair a silver fan in the water. It was Charles and Helen Wainwright. He was humming to her. How beautiful they were. A different kind of marriage, Julia thought, as rare as unicorns.

"Sometimes you can hear this *click, click* he does with his beak," William said, still looking toward the trees. "He can spot a mouse from fifty feet up, at night. Magnificent bird."

Owl, she added to her list, *Wainwright.*

William was silent then. Scanning the sky, listening.

Long moments passed. And then she said, "Have you ever heard of the Gaia theory, William?"

"Gaia?"

"That the earth is a single living organism? It's from Greek mythology, the word, anyway. Gaia, the mother goddess."

She amazed him, gentle, childlike almost, a kind of wistfulness about her, and then out of the blue, scientific theory. How rare was that? Women did not come to him for intelligent conversation. It never occurred to them.

"Makes sense to me," he said. "It's constantly in motion. Volcanoes, earthquakes, weather patterns. The earth turning itself inside out, like shedding skin. And if you look at it logically, wouldn't the source of life have to be alive itself?" He glanced at a leafy philodendron hanging over the water. "Take dirt," he said. "Who thinks of dirt as alive? Yet it grows everything."

"Exactly." She sat up, facing him, her eyes serious. "And you know what I think? If the earth is alive," she cupped her hands as if holding an invisible globe, "and it has this molten core with all these minerals feeding underground lakes . . ." she looked up at him, "then wouldn't places like this where it opens out be special?" Holy, she wanted to say, but that seemed too far, although there were people in the world who believed that. The Japanese built shrines where underground springs bubbled up. "So this could be a kind of gateway to the center," she went on, "the earth's heart. You might even say *soul*, if it's alive."

And if the earth is alive, she thought, then water is its blood. Our blood too. Our bodies mostly water. Maybe that explained what was happening to her here. She splayed her fingers, drew them through the water, felt the silkiness, the ripples against her chest. Water, the universal conductor, carrying the slightest vibration. Was that it? This special water was effecting the water in her body, calling to it, changing it. Sounded crazy, and yet . . .

She glanced past William toward where the owl had disappeared into the trees. "I mean, the animals seem to sense something different," she said. "Maybe that's why they come here, and . . . and odd things happen." She wanted to tell him about her visions. Ralph always said she saw too much, things that weren't there. But not literally, never literally. Until here, in this place. Or maybe it was her mind slipping.

William noticed the change, her eyes almost frightened. He pulled her onto his chest so she was lying full length on top of him. He rubbed her back. "Or it could be just an oasis." He brushed a wisp of hair from her face. "And you can't go by roadrunners. They're always doing weird things."

"But every oasis doesn't have water like this. Feel." She sprinkled handfuls onto his shoulder. Those shoulders, his luscious skin. No, she couldn't tell him. He might think her silly or worse. And what was the point? She was leaving after tomorrow anyway. The thought made her throat catch.

He took her hand, put it to his mouth, sucked her fingers as if to taste the water. "Mmm, yes, minerals," he whispered. "And I like thinking the earth is alive. A goddess. We're lying on her lap right now."

She felt his erection throb against her belly, lifting her in the water. She laughed. And his mouth on her fingertips, that instant pulsing between her legs. Sacred all right, awakening nerve endings she'd almost forgotten she had.

"I have an idea," William said, "we'll write a grant. We'll do a study of mineral springs around the world, observe the wildlife for odd behavior. Publish it in some esoteric journal. It'll take years."

He kissed her, and then in a motion one can only do in water, he turned, slid her onto his back. "But first," he said, nodding to the darker corridor that led to the shallow pool, "let's go over there around the corner for a little odd behavior of our own. Slow and quiet."

She whispered against his neck, breathing his skin. "And naked."

Twenty-one

She was sleeping so peacefully, the sheet pulled up around her face like a child. He had dozed awhile himself, was tempted to stay. But that was one rule he would not bend. Complete, unequivocal, NEVER STAY THE NIGHT. If there was anything he'd learned from women, it was how they hated morning-afters. How, even the first few times with a lover, they'd hardly sleep, then tiptoe to the bathroom to remake themselves before daylight.

And he was not Julia's lover, no matter how it felt. Man, he thought, he'd had plenty of sex in hot tubs and Jacuzzis, but never quite like that, the way she took him in her mouth, like a mermaid devouring her lucky sailor—what a way to die! Then she pulled him down, completely submerged, wrapped her legs and arms around him, moving, until they had to breathe. He'd have given an arm for a snorkel.

William smiled, slipped from the bed, gathered his pants and shirt. He did not stop to look at her again in the soft glow of the moon through the stained glass, her hair still wet on the pillow. No, better not. It was way too easy to be drawn into her fantasy. Not good. He knew too well how reality was always waiting to bite you in the ass. A hired gun, that's all he was. Face it.

In the bathroom, he dressed quickly, tucked in his shirt. He was supposed to come back tomorrow morning between ten and eleven. Now he wasn't sure. Even the chance to drive a Lamborghini Murcielago wasn't worth getting mind-fucked. Not that she was doing it on purpose. Of course not, but if someone rolls a semi over your head by accident, you're still dead.

He saw it now. Julia was the most dangerous of all women. The kind you couldn't forget. The kind to make you lose control completely. Wind up writing poetry, picking wild-flowers, going down on one knee and talking unborn-children-in-her-eyes. And not for the sake of romancing her, but because you couldn't help it. Like an alien takes over your body. That's how it had been with Linda. Until she found out about his "work."

Shit! He had gone too long with the numbness, that's all. A hazard of the trade, build a shell to keep yourself from feeling. Only it starts to calcify inward. Like that high-end call girl he'd met once in the lounge of the Ritz-Carlton. Deborah was the name she used, didn't look at all like a hooker, more like a CEO in a narrow-waisted suit, except he'd never seen a CEO with legs like hers. He smiled, remembering. That was classic, two professionals maneuvering for the proposition. They'd have canceled each other out, except her fee was more, and neither of them was about to pay for sex. When they realized what was happening, they could hardly stop laughing. Deborah's "date" (a Hollywood mogul, she wouldn't say who) had been called home for an emergency, left a roll of bills for a flight back to L.A., the room and her inconvenience.

"I got bored," she'd said, "thought I might as well work, try to double my profit. That's how it gets, honey, the monopoly game never stops." They ended up comparing notes over Dom Perignon. That's when he developed his calcification theory. When Deborah let down her "game face," she made Nancy Carlton look like a lamb. "Sometimes," Deborah said, "I just want to cut off some rich bastard's dick and . . ."

She gave a Medusa laugh. His eyes widened. Then as if to reassure him, "Oh, it's different with you, honey. You're a man. You get to fuck women."

But now he wondered, is that what was happening, his soul trying to chisel through the calcium so he could feel again? And Julia was the catalyst.

He'd been standing at the bathroom sink, zoning. Now he turned, walked back through the room, closed the door quietly behind him.

Just as the latch clicked, he remembered his goodie case on the chair by the bed. Never even opened it. A thousand dollars' worth of tools, at least. Batteries alone . . .

He tried the door. Locked tight. Fuck!

Twenty-two

William lit a cigarette and was halfway up the path when he heard the *click*, *click* and froze as the white owl swooped down onto the grass, grabbed something in its talons. It cocked its head, and those big owl eyes stared at him for a split second. He half expected it to say, "Who?" A lizard wriggled under its foot. Then it launched and flew off toward the trees.

Man! Not twenty feet from him. His heart beating faster, just the surprise of it. How big it was, close up. Protection or a dark omen. He felt something like a shiver run through him, shrugged it off.

In the parking lot, he couldn't help circling the Lamborghini again, slowly. An engineering marvel, all right. Gave new meaning to the word *sleek*, gleaming in the night, a kind of life of its own. He laughed. Julia and her theories. Gaia. He'd tell her about the owl.

Maybe forgetting his goodie case wasn't a mistake. He had to come back. It was okay. No more delusions. She was a catalyst, that's all.

In his truck, he checked the time on his cell phone. 12:03. There was a message. He pushed the button, listened.

"It's Erma. I need to see you, Javier. I'll be at our motel tomorrow morning, room four, the usual time."

He lit another cigarette, started his truck. Man, he was tired. Had a right to be.

Erma Smedley. He hadn't heard from her in over a month. The thought of facing Erma Smedley after Julia . . . Okay, not facing. That's not how Erma liked it.

What a case. Mr. and Mrs. Smedley with their six kids, pillars of one of those talking-in-tongues churches up in Yucca Valley. Now, there was a place to study oddness. Yucca Valley was known nationally for its UFO sightings. And locally as a nest of apocalypse nuts, people who fully expected any day to be beamed up, while the unsaved got their heads lopped off by fiery swords. Families who sold all their possessions for an end-of-the-world celebration every ten years or so. Like a high school reunion.

He drove past the gatehouse, turned toward Palm Springs, smoking to stay awake. Usual time, Erma said. Seven forty-five Sunday morning. He could be back at Hidden Springs by ten, easy. Erma never took more than a half hour. She had it all worked out in advance. Every few weeks she would go alone into the desert to meditate before the Sunday service. That's what she told her family, anyway. So when she walked in a little late and took her seat in the choir loft, no one questioned the look of rapture on her face.

He did not want to go tomorrow. He could just say he didn't get the message. That option set much better in his gut. To see Erma Smedley, then an hour later, Julia . . . the thought actually made him queasy, almost like betrayal.

In his headlights a shape appeared from the side of the road. He braked as a coyote loped across, then disappeared behind a creosote bush. There was her coyote. He would tell her. Maybe they'd see one tomorrow on their drive.

Betrayal. What the hell was he thinking? It was a job. You don't leave one job until you find another, savings or no savings. If he started skipping appointments, he *would* be out of control. Dead in the water. Julia lived in Minnesota; he'd known her six hours. A catalyst, that's all.

Besides, the good thing about Erma was she preferred toys. And if the spares were still in the bottom drawer of his desk, he was home free.

Twenty-three

Indio Boulevard. Javier tilted the visor against the glare of the morning sun as he turned off I-10. Erma Smedley needed help, he decided, far more than he could give her. There were plenty of places she could've chosen without driving twenty-five miles farther to Indio. In a row of smutty motels Erma wanted the smuttiest. It wasn't that she couldn't afford better. You had to be indigent not to afford better.

The stench of mildew, stale cigarettes, crack pipes and someone else's sex turned her on. Or maybe it was the mystique. Besides hookers and heroin addicts, Indio Boulevard was known for bringing down the famed TV evangelist, Jimmy Swaggart, in the '80s. Poor Jimmy, pulled over by a rookie cop, a prostitute in the passenger seat eager to confess. On national television, as it turned out.

Javier drove past the boarded-up Denny's, then the slab and capped pipes that had been the old Arco. On his left, a mile-long freight train was rolling to a stop, boxcars banging their couplings. His great-grandfather came up from Jalisco in 1911 to work the Southern Pacific. When Palm Springs was little more than ruts in the sand, Indio had been a railroad hub, serving thousands of acres of ranches, cattle yards and citrus growers and those pioneer farmers who brought back dates from Arabia. The whole east valley had once been blanketed with groves. Grandma Estella still lived six blocks over in Sun Gold, the first housing tract to take out an entire orchard, but in 1948 builders left as many trees as possible, and from the air Sun Gold still looked like a hundred-acre date grove.

Much of the farming was gone now, businesses moved to strip malls on the outskirts, and no amount of city council beautification plans had been able to do much for the downtown, especially Indio Boulevard.

He drove under the overpass. Sunday morning, not a soul on the street, not even the old guy with his wagon and team of dogs, elaborate harnesses woven from baling twine, canvas bags bulging against the slats, like he was off to the Yukon instead of scavenging empty cans. Or Marla, the black prostitute; he didn't see her either. Marla had actually been a fashion model, 'til her boyfriend took a knife to her face. She still walked as if she were on a runway, shoulders back, hand on her hip, mumbling, her hair all sponged out. He'd seen her a couple of mornings, walking home after her last trick, he supposed.

He turned into the parking lot of the Cactus Inn, an L-shaped single-story building, twelve rooms, faded yellow walls. Jaundice yellow, he called it. He pulled up beside Erma's Honda SUV. There were no other cars. People who used this motel did not own cars.

The queasiness was back in his gut. He did not want to be here. But what was he supposed to do? He hadn't slept much, thinking of Julia. Six hours, and he couldn't stop seeing her lying there in the glow from the skylight, her hair wet on the pillow, the sheet pulled up . . . Shit. Catalyst, that's all.

He grabbed his shaving kit which held his few spare "tools" and got out. Had to step over debris from what looked like a curb party, empty bottles and paper cups, two forty-ounce Red Dogs, greasy AM/PM wrappers, a hypodermic needle. Christ!

He knocked, waited a minute, then tried the knob. It wasn't locked. Not good. He'd told her, always, always lock the door.

That was one reason he'd come; no way to call and tell her he couldn't make it. Erma wasn't his favorite client, but it still bothered him to leave her waiting alone in this motel.

She was sitting in the chair, wearing a version of the same flowered dress as always, lace collar, tiny lavender purse clutched in both hands. All she needed was a veiled hat and gloves, could've walked right out of the '50s.

She was leaning back, her eyes open, staring. Erma did that sometimes, she'd just go quiet, blank, but in this light she looked paler than usual. My God, he thought, what if she's dead? His stomach clenched. He'd heard the stories. The nightmare decision, turn around and leave, or dial 911, face the investigation. Happened to call girls more than people knew, but when a man died in the arms of a whore, the police usually covered it up quickly. A woman might be another story.

"Erma?"

He closed the door, stepped forward. The room was dim from the single bulb over the bed. A window unit clanked and wheezed a few feet from her, mostly recycling the smells. She couldn't hear, probably. The room stank even more than he remembered, a hint of vomit mixed in with the rest, a film of Lysol only making it worse.

"Erma?"

He didn't see any blood, no gun. Pills maybe. If she was

dead, it wouldn't be natural causes, not if half of what she'd told him was true.

Finally she turned toward him, and he felt a wave of relief, then surprise. She'd been crying, although her eyes were dry now, and on her face was a look he'd never seen before. Anguish, despair, so raw and dark that it would propel her to this room and what she paid him to do. It was like watching someone trying to absorb the worst possible news; there's been an accident, a terrible accident. And then her eyes focused on him, and the look was gone, covered instantly with her get-through-the-day face.

"You're late," she said over the noise and sputter of the air conditioner. "We'll have to hurry. Where's your case? You didn't forget it, did you?"

The tone she used getting six teenagers ready for church, he imagined. "Snap, snap, no argument, you're going." But he didn't give a damn what tone she used. As long as that look was gone. Dead was better than that look.

He forced some lightness into his own voice. "I brought a few specialties," he said, "just came in the mail." He sat on the sunken mattress, his knees almost touching hers, unzipped his shaving kit.

She peered in as if choosing from a box of chocolates.

"Well, now, well . . ." Her face lit up. "This one. Yes, definitely!"

Twenty-four

Of course, he thought. The Three-Pronged Pearl Butterfly Dancer. Most extravagant love toy he'd ever seen, excluding the life-sized blowup numbers. The Pearl Butterfly Dancer had six different speeds, each prong had its own controls and could be bent gently to the desired angle. The clear "flesh-like" shaft was filled with dozens of pearls that turned slowly at the first notch on the main dial. At max speed it rotated three hundred sixty degrees twenty-four times, then reversed automatically. Set him back $184.98, batteries not included.

The thing even had a remote control option which baffled

him, at first. What, so husbands could keep watching TV, handle the wife from across the room? How's that honey? When you're done could you bring me another Bud?

Designed more for solitary amusement, of course. He imagined some geeky engineer bent over a desk drafting these contraptions. Female geek, probably. He'd had to practice awhile to get the controls down. That was the reason he'd been a few minutes late.

But he could see Erma had already forgiven him completely. She didn't even wait to get to the bed. The moment he took it out of the case, she turned, bent over the chair, hiked up her skirt revealing black fishnet stockings, black satin garter belt, and crotch-less panties. Those were new. Must've put them on when she got here, would remove them before church, he presumed, at least the stockings.

"You like?" she said, grinning at him over her shoulder.

He nodded, mumbled approval, trying to remember which damn dial did what. Easier to concentrate back in his apartment without Erma right there in that position, eager.

He turned the switch too far and the thing practically jumped out of his hands. $184.98, you'd think they could make it quieter. He'd write a letter.

There. Got it. Okay, here we go.

She came in about a minute and a half, then again and

again. No rules about screaming in this motel. One good thing, anyway.

But what happened next caught him completely off balance. Her sudden silence might've warned him, if he hadn't been busy trying to shut the thing off. Instead of collapsing, she went rigid, her hands tightened on the arms of the chair, then her shoulders began to heave violently, and she started to sob, almost wail, loud animal cries that could freeze blood.

He reached to somehow console her when suddenly she whirled, and the back of her hand struck his jaw hard, knocking him to the bed. Erma Smedley was not a small woman, but even at half her size, with that fury she couldn't've tossed a refrigerator.

She came at him, face contorted, that look again, only worse, hideous, tears streaming, and even as he lay stunned he registered how insane this was, scrambling onto the bed in her flowered Sunday dress with the lace collar, those fishnet stockings.

She retrieved the still buzzing toy, grabbed his belt. "You," she screamed, "now, you! The way you like it, up the fucking ass, you bastard! Faggot! You goddamned fucking son of a bitch faggot!"

She was over him, tugging at his belt, almost lifting him. He managed to get hold of one wrist and twist. She dropped the vibrator. Then she wrenched her hand away, landed another blow, this time to his eye. He felt the skin break. Shit!

He used his full strength now, heaved her off of him, then straddled her, pinned her arms.

"Erma . . . Erma," he said, shaking her, his voice firm, at the same time gentle. "Look at me, Erma. I'm not him. Do you hear me? Do you understand? I am not him!"

Twenty-five

When Julia opened her eyes, she felt a wash of contentment; William was there, lying beside her. She did not remember falling asleep, didn't even remember coming back to the room. The grotto pool she remembered. Oh, yes. Flesh on flesh in the water, smooth, like dolphins mating, only dolphins had no hands, no legs to wrap around.

He was facing away from her, the sheet slung across his hip. She did not move, but with her eyes she traced the contour of his back and shoulder, the rise and fall of his breathing. His skin that beautiful brown. The exact shade skin is supposed to be, she decided. How people worked to have skin that color, tanning booths and creams. He was sleeping so gently. She would not wake him. Stay perfectly still. If only she could levitate, drift silently up, so she could see his face.

It surprised her when, in the next moments, she did just that. Well, not exactly that. More like an out-of-body experience, yet so simple, really, slipping out of herself as easily as taking off a coat. A lifting sensation beneath her back, like bubbles rising in water, only much slower. A soul follows its own course more slowly, she thought, but still follows. It must. Like water finding its way. Everything is like water. No mistakes, no sins, only water.

She floated upward, inch by inch. An almost overwhelming sense of joy, that something supposedly impossible was such a breeze. "The unbearable lightness of being"; she hadn't a clue what that meant until now. Weightlessness. Essence. Achieved only by distillation, reduction to the purest elements, oxygen, hydrogen. Water. Love was like water, or should be, flowing naturally wherever it willed, finite, yet infinitely changing. To truly live you must know the lightness. Like vapor.

What a feeling, drifting, rising, free. She wanted to keep going, maybe move on up through the skylight, head toward Saturn. But William. William was the reason. Without William she would never have found how easy it was.

Like a large catfish she hovered just below the stained glass lily pads, looked down. She could see them both lying there, peaceful as puppies. How beautiful they were, dark and light, framed by swirls of sheet, mottled colors from the skylight splashed here and there, shimmering on their closed lids. Like a painting: *Sunday Morning Lovers*.

It was the ticking that ruined it. Broke through, made her remember. The clock, time. Half gone already. Another twenty-four hours starting to tick away. Hurry. She lost her grip and fell back into her body with a sickening thud.

A moment to clear the dizziness, then she reached and touched William's shoulder. They must hurry, take what time was left, now. But when he turned, it was not William at all, but Ralph. Laughing at her, like Banquo's ghost, mocking. Silly woman. Did you think I wouldn't find you?

She woke shaking, gripping the sheet, the bed empty beside her.

Twenty-six

Julia curled into a ball, pulled the sheet tight around her. Hands over her face, shaking, heart out of control, like a child hiding from nightmares. Why would her mind conjure such a dream? Euphoric images only to trick her, make the plunge back to reality worse.

Well, she was not a child. She was not crazy. It was just a dream. And there are infinite realities. You could choose, couldn't you? Tomorrow she would retrace her steps, drive to L.A., walk onto the plane. At home she would sit with Ralph and . . . What? Suggest counseling? Right, some pin-head psychologist, he'd say. But they needed to get it clear, what they both wanted for their lives now that the kids were gone. Each make a list, maybe compare. Talk this out, before the years slipped away, each the same as the last.

What did Ralph want? she wondered. Besides his business, and a damn hunting lodge on Muskeg Bay? Oh, if they started that conversation. I had a right to know! How could you not tell me? After what I did for you? Pathetic. A soap opera script. She never even confronted him about the papers she'd found that day in his desk. At least in silence there was some dignity.

No, she would not fall into blaming. Letting someone choose for you is a choice in itself. "No wife of mine is going to work," he'd said. And the truth was, staying home with the children all those years was a luxury, a blessing. Who wouldn't want to be home with her babies? The sweet contentment of not having to juggle career, babysitters, negotiating days off when the children were sick. Quiet hours rocking and nursing each one, reading them stories. She loved that. Playing with them as they grew, and, yes, surviving their traumas. Like labor, you forget the bad parts. Then when Janet, their youngest, started kindergarten, all those midday hours to read through her personal library, before the flurry of after-school activities. Soccer mom. She'd become a voting block!

And suddenly the house was empty, Elizabeth married in

Cleveland, Janet in her second year at Columbia. Matthew off with a bluegrass band in West Virginia. Ralph still grumbled about that. "Momma's boy, degree in music, where the hell will that get you? Damned hippy." He'd wanted his son to take over the business.

Julia curled tighter on the bed. A hunting lodge, and her name not even on the deed. $489,000, nearly half a million, imagine where you could go on that kind of money.

She thought of her grandfather's house, one of the oldest in St. Paul, built in 1875, three stories. Polished oak banisters, cherrywood wainscoting, doors with hand-tooled brass hinges. Window seats in the front parlor lined with cedar. As a girl, she had sat there reading, wrapped in her great grandmother's crazy quilt which was nearly as old as the house, velvet and satin patches, burgundy, deep blues and browns, old choir robes and drapes, suit linings. Even now the smell of cedar took her back to those bay windows.

When her grandfather died, Ralph advised them to sell the house, no sense keeping it, and she handed him her half to start the business, paid for that first diesel Mack. 1979. Just like that, her entire inheritance. She might've traveled some, with Lucille if Ralph wouldn't go.

Blaming. There it was. As hard as you try not to . . . Stupid! As if she weren't even an accomplice in her own life. She turned onto her back, closed her eyes.

No, there was no point in talking or making lists. It was clear what Ralph would want. Ralph would want that girl she had been at twenty, before the babies. Before she retreated into her books. The girl who'd sat with him in a duck blind, shivering under all those layers, waiting for sunrise and the cacophony of a flock answering that silly horn he had her squawk out over the decoys. Trying not to giggle. Teasing, nuzzling his stubbly neck. Come on, it'll warm us up. We can manage. I put on my long johns backwards.

When you're young you think if you please him enough he will take the time to know you, know how to please you back.

Where was that girl? she wondered. Who followed him across yellow fields crackling with frost, watching for the flush of patridges. "My bird dog," he called her when she cooked up feasts for the crew. She refused to be one of those wives who wait at home chatting with the neighbor ladies about whatever preserves they were putting up that day. And it was true; there is nothing quite like watching hundreds of snow geese lift off a lake in the morning sun.

But by the time Matthew was born she knew she'd twisted the head off her last bird.

Was that the difference? Men simply want more of the same, keep what you have, hold life tight to your vest, own things. More trucks and crews. A hunting lodge. While women wish for all they've never seen or touched. Fling it aside and run. Paris. No, more exotic. Carnival in Rio, plumes and sequined masks, people dancing the samba.

No, it wasn't so simple, had nothing to do with gender. There was a certain physics in marriage. Like one of those desk games, steel balls on strings, that clack against each other. One partner's change propels the other with precisely the same force in the opposite direction.

She thought of that night almost twenty years ago. Matthew was a toddler. He'd had one of his screaming ear infections, and she rocked and rocked him. Even when he finally slept, she kept holding him, so beautiful, there in the dark, only the red glow of his clown night-light. And the rustle of the books multiplying on the shelves behind her, books and more books, floor-to-ceiling shelves already full in the next room, guarding Elizabeth as she slept, almost five years old.

Another baby. She hadn't told anyone.

"Are you all right? You want me to take him?" Ralph knelt beside the rocker, his face soft in the reddish light. In his voice, a tenderness he had not used before or since. She could not answer. Her plans might spill out.

"You aren't happy, are you?" He touched her cheek. "I've seen it. If you just tell me what you want, I . . ."

He waited.

Still, she could not speak. Such hurt in his eyes. Her fault. Thinking she could live such a life and nothing more. He was letting her go. "Tell me what you want . . ." What she wanted was courage. She would get an abortion, was it so wrong? Her body. She would find a good sitter, a job, anything until a teaching position opened up.

Ralph's next words were so low she had to lean forward. "You won't have the children, you know." He stood, lifted Matthew from her arms, set him in his crib. The sudden emptiness was a cold wave pushing her back, air sucked from her chest. But when Ralph turned, his eyes had changed completely, the hurt set aside, like a lever thrown, tracks sliding into place, brief repair, that's all. She stared, wondering if she'd heard right.

"City manager over in Stillwater approved the bid," he said. "Snow removal. No more scrimping through the winter." He smiled. "I booked the cabin on the Cheyenne River for antelope season. Four of the guys are going, so far. Tom's still deciding. I thought you might want to come. The kids too, why not? Pete says he'll cook, so it wouldn't be like before . . ."

"I'm pregnant," she said, before she could stop the words. Shit! Alone all day in that sod roof cabin, no running water or electricity, no indoor toilet. Matthew still in diapers. All right. This is how decisions are made. And the inefficiency of a tiny coil. All right.

In twenty years they never once mentioned that night. Nor had she ever again seen that look in Ralph's eyes.

"All right," she said out loud, staring up at the colored glass. So what about her list? What did she want now? At first she'd thought of volunteering at the city library, no reason to stay home, and maybe reverse her system, go backwards from the 900s, for every nonfiction book, two novels, like dessert . . .

Or maybe she'd just have dessert.

Julia stretched out on the empty space where William had been, breathed his scent. No, it wasn't the dream that bothered her so much. It wasn't Ralph's mocking face or the decisions still to be made. It was that William didn't stay. She'd thought he would stay.

Twenty-seven

J ulia wasn't in the cabin. Three times he knocked and waited, thinking she might be still asleep or in the shower. Maybe she was at the pool. He started down the path to the grotto, then turned back. He found Charles Wainwright's business card in his pocket, wrote a note, pried one edge under the number on the door.

"I'm a little early," the note said, "if you come back before I find you, stay here. Okay?" He signed it *William*.

She wasn't in the pool or by the lake or in the restaurant. He hurried back to the cabin. Wainwright's card was still on the door. For a moment he felt a kind of constriction in his chest, but, no, she was here, somewhere. The Lamborghini was in the parking lot.

He checked all three places again, thinking she might be one step ahead of him, then walked out beyond the restaurant to the saltwater pool. He scanned the guests lounging under the *palapas*, didn't see her. Maybe the spa.

The lady at the desk checked her appointment book. "Julia. Oh, yes, the Clay Cabana." She gave him directions. Across the grass behind the spa, a row of treatment decks looked out over the gardens. "You'll see the sign," she said.

He went out the back, across the thick lawn. He parted the first curtain. A woman was lying in one of the cement troughs, submerged to her chin in a loamy mud. Her back was to him, a white towel wrapped in a turban on her head.

He entered quietly, and only when he saw it was Julia did he realize how anxious he'd been. Even his breathing changed. There it was, he thought, the test of true beauty. Her hair bound up, face coated with mud, masking all but her eyes, which were closed. How lovely the shape of her face, her cheekbones.

He should be careful, she might not want him here. He knew how women were about being caught in mid-tune-up, mysteries exposed, but he could not leave. He sat on the edge of the cement trough, breathing the earthy scent of peat and reddish clay. It blended with tamarisk and creosote and Texas sage. One side of the cabana was open to a rustic garden and the desert and mountains beyond.

She must've sensed him watching her, opened her eyes.

"William, oh . . ." She sat up a little, a faint sucking sound as her shoulders and breasts came up out of the mud. "William," she said again, her face lighting up even through the mud, then her smile disappeared. "My God, what happened to your eye? Are you okay?" She pulled a hand free, lifted it toward him.

"It's nothing . . ." he said, touching the bandage, trying not to stare at her breasts, little clumps of mud sliding off, but before he could decide just how much to tell her, the curtain opened, and a young woman came in.

"Is everything all right, Miss Reeves?"

She came forward briskly as if to assess what was happening here. People didn't just walk in, especially fully dressed, like entering a Neiman Marcus in a ski mask. In his search for Julia, he'd gotten more than one suspicious look. He could imagine the call to the office. A man is lurking about the grounds, and he's wearing clothes!

"Yes, just fine," Julia said. "Heather, this is William. He's my guest." Julia glanced at the other trough a foot away. "Maybe he'd like a treatment too. Could you tell them at the desk?" She squirmed her shoulders back under the mud, smiled up at him. "You really should try it, William."

"Well, sure, of course," Heather said, apologizing with her eyes. "I'll leave another towel on the bench. You can explain how to get in?"

Julia nodded.

When Heather closed the curtain behind her, Julia's voice changed, and she held him with her smile. "Oh, William, I had a dream that you stayed. It was so real, and then . . . but now you're here. I'm so glad." She hesitated a moment as if considering the clumsy process of extricating herself from the mud and washing off so she could kiss him. Then she nodded to the bandage above his eye.

"Tell me. Tell me what happened."

Twenty-eight

All the way from the motel he had been thinking what to tell Julia. No, even before, while he still had Erma pinned on the bed. What finally snapped Erma out was the blood dripping from his split eyebrow onto her face. "Get off," she'd said, "you'll stain my dress," and when he released her wrists and rolled onto his back, she scurried into the bathroom.

He thought she might bring him a towel, but in moments she came out all smoothed and proper again. She collected her purse, dropped the fishnet stockings into the wastebasket and left. Along with the Pearl Butterfly Dancer, he discovered minutes later on his way out.

He had to hold a washcloth over his eye as he drove. Not until he stopped at the nearest Urgent Care Center, where they stitched and bandaged the cut, did he realize Erma hadn't paid him either. Two clients chalked off in a single weekend.

And now Julia looking up at him from the mud with those raccoon eyes.

"Well, it's kind of a long story," he said.

"Then you probably should get in first." Julia glanced at the other trough. "I'm already half through. It gets pretty hot, you can only stand it so long."

Sweat was making rivulets in the thin layer of mud on her cheeks. She pulled a hand out, then realized she could hardly wipe her face with it.

William stood, slipped off his clothes and shoes, set them on the bench a few feet away. Through a doorway was a large shower cubicle open to the sky. He crossed the wood plank floor, wet one end of a towel and walked back to her.

She grinned, taking in his naked body. "Oh, my gosh," she said.

He laughed. "You're starting to look like an alluvial plain." He sat on the wide edge of her trough, dabbed her forehead. "Want me to wipe it all off, or just the drips?"

"All," she said, closing her eyes. He wiped them carefully, then her cheeks. It took another trip back to the shower to wash out the end of the towel and get the rest. He could feel her eyes on him as he walked back and forth. A plastic cup of ice water was on the ledge behind her head. He reached across, held the straw to her lips.

"Better now?"

She nodded. "Much."

He leaned, kissed her. She arched to him, her nipples surfacing again. She tasted of minerals, clay. He felt himself get hard, wanted to lift her out, take her here on the plank floor, but there was still her question.

He stood, surveyed the other trough. "Okay, how do I do this?"

"Well, the bottom is very hot," she said, as if speaking to his erect penis. "So you don't step in." She forced her eyes upward, smiling. "Sit on the edge, hold the bar and lower yourself, butt first. It's so buoyant you have to work yourself down, but not too far. The mud forms exactly to your body, like Styrofoam packing." She laughed, watching as he followed the instructions.

"Man," he said. It surprised him, how the mud held his body suspended for a few seconds, then he started to sink. It felt strange, being drawn gradually down, cushioned, the rich loamy scent filling his lungs. A bit unnerving, too, like being sucked into a bog. He was resisting the instinct to struggle free when he noticed his dick standing up from the mud like the neck of a clam. He glanced at Julia to see if she'd noticed. She had, and then their eyes met and they were laughing like little kids, uncontrolled bursts, eyes filling with tears as they watched the "clam" fold over and disappear.

He leaned his head back on the folded towel, still chuckling. They were quiet a minute or two. He looked out the open space to the garden, the sun washing color from the lavender mountains. It was that cusp time between morning and full-on day, the desert giving up its freshness, the last traces of moisture sucked from creosote and sage and brittlebush, bracing for the coming heat.

No reason to lie, William thought. Julia was a client too. And she was leaving tomorrow. He touched the gauze bandage above his eye.

"Well," he began, casually, "I had an appointment this morning."

Twenty-nine

Julia listened. What else could she do, trapped here in the mud? She had expected maybe a barroom scuffle or a run-in with a door, the benevolent lie. Certainly not an attack by a deranged client. Fourteen stitches, he said. Church lady from hell.

An appointment! This morning as she was waking up, as she was dreaming her silly dream. Julia breathed in. Ridiculous, to feel this way, her heart accelerating stupidly. It was his job. Not as if she had commandeered his every minute. Although she might have made it clear, paid him extra to stay. Paid. How ugly that sounded. Almost as ugly as picturing him in some sleazy motel with . . .

No, Julia thought, breathe, control it. Problem was, she'd been trying to act like a man, "paying for it," yet still thinking like a woman. All she'd wanted was simple, unattached passion. Okay, lust, raw sex. A business transaction. But, no, she couldn't just leave it at that, had to decorate it with ribbons and bows, fucking rose petals. Romance. There was the killer. Next, you disappear. Hell, she couldn't even get her fantasies straight. Pay to fuck her blind, then expect him to stay and cuddle in the morning. Stupid. Get over it.

"I usually make it a rule never to talk about a client," William was saying, "but then I never had one split my head open before." He chuckled. He'd kept the story to a minimum, anyway. No background details. No Three-Pronged Pearl Butterfly Dancer.

Julia did not look at him. She pulled her hands from the mud, but could do little but rub her fingers and thumbs together, watch the ooze.

William wished he could see her face better, her eyes, sunk to his neck in this damn trough, sweat dripping into his bandage. She was too quiet, hadn't spoken a word since he'd started.

"Julia? Are you all right?"

Nothing. She seemed to be studying the texture of the mud, her mind far away. Was that a smile starting or was she trying not to cry?

My God, Julia thought, how could she miss such a chance? Think what she could learn from him. What brought these women to him, what exactly did they ask for? Did they want threesomes sometimes? Did he have a colleague he called in for backup? Costumes? She imagined him as a professor, tweed jacket, leather patches at the elbows; she'd sit in front of him on his big desk, undo his tie, remove his wire-framed glasses, slide her legs over his shoulders, an Oxford dictionary under her butt.

Oh, my gosh, yes, she would pay him to tell her his stories. She felt a surge of . . . was it power? A release from illusion? Like walking out in the middle of a Disney movie.

"Look, Julia," William was saying, "I didn't mean to upset you. I guess it's a rule I shouldn't break. I should've made something up . . ."

"No, go on, tell me." She turned to him. "I want to know more. Why did she hire you? What made her so angry? What made her snap?"

There was almost a glint in her eyes, a hardness. Calcification, William thought, be careful. But it was tempting, if she meant it. In three years, he had never told anyone, except that evening with Deborah, the high-class hooker. Shop talk. And even then, he'd mostly listened.

"Well," William started, "the woman has plenty of reason to come unglued."

Thirty

He went on carefully, never using Erma Smedley's name. How she had married at nineteen, a man ten years older, they had six children. How her husband kept an apartment above his insurance agency in Palm Springs for when his "appointments" ran late. William paused. "Then, about a year ago," he said, "a boy from their church youth group told his parents that Mr. . . . , that her husband, took him there one night." He lowered his voice, "Gave him drugs, sodomized him . . . other things. Kid had to hitchhike home, all the way to Yucca Valley at four a.m. His

parents were frantic, so the boy made up a story at first, a friend's car broke down." William spoke quickly. "Anyway, the charges wouldn't hold in court. His word against an adult's. The boy was almost eighteen, and their attorney found kids at his high school to testify that he was gay."

"Was he?" Julia said. This was not at all what she expected. She had asked, but my God!

"Hardly matters," William said. "If the kid was the slightest bit different, there are always teenagers who'd say that. Anyway, they couldn't prove it wasn't consensual. The guy got off."

Julia braced on the sides of the trough, raised up, the air cooling her shoulders. She thought of the woman. "But six children," she said, "all that time. How could she not know?"

"Well, they had an image in the community," William said. "They were very big in their church. Are, I should say. After the scandal, he stood in front of the congregation and told about his struggle over the years, but he swore he never touched the boy. They laid hands on him."

Julia nodded. Oh, she knew about images. She had nowhere to stand on images. Mildred Jensen was filling in for her Sunday school class right now, or a few hours ago, considering the time difference. She felt queasy.

"But I meant personally," she said, "sexually. There had to be signs. Even if you're in denial, you get glimmers. But I guess it wasn't her husband's fault. He was trapped too, don't you think?"

William heard the tremor in her voice, didn't answer.

They were silent for several moments. The locust hum, a warm breeze stirring the tamarisks. The mud getting too hot to stand. William nodded, closed his eyes. When he spoke again, it was almost to himself. "'The hypocrite's crime is that he bears false witness to himself.'"

"What?"

"It's a quote," he said, "someone we studied in Twentieth Century Philosophy. A woman," he said, thinking. "Holocaust survivor. I can't remember her name."

Julia stared at him. He really was a philosophy major. She felt guilty that she hadn't believed him, but it fit, the way he talked sometimes.

"She believed evil results from the failure of rationality." William shook his head, looking up at the sky. "Damn, what was her name?"

"Hannah Arendt," she said softly.

He looked at her, stunned. "Yes, Hannah Arendt. How did you know?"

She smiled. It felt good to smile. "Well, there aren't too many women philosophers from the forties. I read. A lot."

There was an understatement. In a few moments she said, "So what happened to the boy?"

William hesitated. "Oh, it isn't . . ."

"No, go on," she said, "you can't stop now."

"He . . . well, a few weeks after the case was dismissed, he committed suicide."

Thirty-one

William saw his mistake as soon as the words were out.

Julia put her hand to her mouth. "Oh. Oh, no." She thought of her own son, Matthew, the day he left, banjo case flung across his back, the other instruments already in the van. He set down his suitcases, hugged her, there in the drive, patting her back the way he'd done since he was a baby. "Momma's boy." Ralph wasn't there to see him off.

"Tell Dad I said good-bye."

To lose a child for something so . . .

Julia looked down at the mud encasing her, stifling . . . She could hardly breathe. "I have to get out. I have to go. Now!"

William watched as she struggled, her eyes filling with tears. She was forgetting the procedure, would scald her feet on the bottom. In one movement, he grabbed the bar, wrenched himself out. He braced his knees on the side of her trough, worked his arms under her legs and back. Where he found the strength to lift her against the suction of the mud, he would never know, but he did. And luckily she didn't fight him, but leaned against his chest, crying.

"I'm sorry," he said, "I'm sorry." This was his fault. They only think they want to know. Protected all her life, probably.

He carried her, thinking how they must look, naked, covered with slime, dripping clumps onto the floor. Afraid she'd slide right out of his arms, he adjusted his grip. He felt something pop in his back, and his right knee throbbed. Damn football years. "*Shh*, it's all right. It's all right."

She wasn't just crying for the boy. He knew that.

He walked slowly, carefully, across the planks to the shower room, had to concentrate on every step not to slip, limping slightly. Like a horror movie, *Mummy Takes a Bride*. At the rubber mat, he looked up at the shower head, helpless. Didn't want to disturb her cry. He took another step, bent a little, maybe he could turn it on with his fingertips, but no, his knee started to wobble.

"Julia, ah . . . do you think you could reach the knob?"

She lifted her head from his chest, looked around, dazed, as if not sure how she got there. "What? Oh." She leaned, turned it on, but as she did the towel wrapped around her head slipped off. "Shit. Oh, my gosh. Don't look at me!"

William tried not to smile. Her hair crushed and spiked all crazy, like a punk rocker who'd slept wrong.

She wriggled out of his arms and stepped into the spray. Ridiculous, she thought, one minute crying for how sick and senseless it all was, the next worrying how she looked.

She closed her eyes, rinsing, lifting her hair to the water. William watched the mud sliding off her shoulders and down her back, the curve of her waist and hips, her skin revealed in patches of white, like alabaster. A marble statue unearthed.

He wasn't sure he should touch her, but there was still mud on her back and legs. He stepped in. "Here, you missed some." He scrubbed with his hands, turning her, directing the spray. And when she rubbed the water from her eyes and saw he was still covered with it, she scrubbed him too, mud swirling at their feet.

It took a long time. Laughing now, pointing out places they'd missed, managing their own crevices and crannies, her sadness dissipating with the task at hand. Had to be done, she thought, although not exactly a chore.

William did not want to get hard, but there was no stopping it, her hands on him, bodies touching, skin wet and silky from the mud and minerals, nudging each other for the spray.

When she saw, she smiled, held him in her hand, stroking. She knelt to take him in her mouth, but he pulled her back up, kissed her, there under the spray. That's all he wanted, to kiss her, take her away.

Completely clean again, water running over their faces, tongues lapping, slurping sounds drowned by the shower. They clung together, and when she asked, he lifted her onto him, ignoring his bad knee, his cut stinging under the wet bandage as she wrapped her legs around him, gripped his shoulders, rocking, kissing between gasps.

Vaguely, he heard a voice coming from the trough room. Something about sheets in ice water, herbal wraps. Over Julia's shoulder, he saw Heather in the doorway, holding a bucket, eyes widening.

"Oops," she said, "sorry . . ."

Thirty-two

Julia's sudden intensity should not have surprised him. The transfer of emotion, sorrow to passion, like making love after a fight. But it was all he could do to stand, holding her as she rocked on him, clutching his shoulders, kissing his mouth and face, gasping, water running over them.

It was a race then, if he could make her come before his knee gave out. When her gasps became yelps he found her mouth, muffled her cries until she relaxed against him, just in time.

Limping, he carried her the few feet to the bench, managed to sit. He held her on his lap, her legs still around his waist. He rubbed her back. Something about her . . . so vulnerable, yet determined. He wanted to shelter her, he wanted to be with her.

Shit. What was he thinking? This time they had was not real. Tomorrow she was leaving. Maybe he'd drive her to L.A., see her off at the airport, catch a flight back to Palm Springs. Jesus, damn knee! He had to stretch out his leg. A groan escaped when he moved.

Julia looked up, smiling contentedly until she saw his eyes. "Oh, William . . ." She unstraddled his lap quickly, sat beside him.

Interesting maneuver, naked. He wasn't in too much pain to appreciate that.

"What?" she said. "Did I hurt you?"

"No, it's nothing. My knee. It'll be better in a few minutes." He leaned back, rotating his foot. "Old football injury, flares up now and then. I'm not getting any younger."

"Oh, yeah. What are you, thirty?"

"Thirty-three," he said, "almost."

She laughed, then slid from the bench, knelt in front of him, her eyes concerned. "Should I rub it?" she said.

"I don't think rubbing's the best idea." He grimaced, holding his thigh.

Julia remembered the time Matthew pulled ligaments

sliding into home plate. She got up, retrieved the towel from the mat, turned off the shower. She brought the ice bucket from the doorway, dunked the towel in with the sheets, then wrapped his knee gently. "There. How's that?" She smiled up at him. "Your knee will smell like lavender and rosemary."

He looked at her, cheeks still flushed from sex, kneeling there, rays of sunlight through the open roof glistening her skin: *Nymph by a Pond*. He couldn't stop thinking of statues, works of art.

"You're so beautiful," he said, "I wish you could see yourself."

She blushed, glanced at her breasts, resisted the urge to cross her arms in front. A moment passed, and she nodded to the bucket. "Shall we wrap in these sheets? We probably shouldn't waste them." She looked up. "We can sit by the garden. I'll help you. You can stretch out on the lounge chair. I'll ask Heather to bring gauze and tape. They must have a first aid kit. Your bandage is soaked, and you're . . . bleeding."

He touched it. There was an ache behind his eye he'd hardly noticed before, concentrating on his knee, and now the cut stung. Fine specimen he was. What could he do, file for workman's comp? Had to be a better way to make a living. He chuckled at the thought, but wasn't at all sure about getting wrapped in a perfumed sheet, especially a freezing one.

"It's just a little blood," Julia said, "but you should have a dry bandage. Then I'll order a picnic lunch, and we'll go for our drive. And later we'll have dinner again on the balcony or maybe by the lake."

She stood, pulled a sheet from the bucket, bits of herbs and petals clinging to it, the aroma blossoming out, strong. She wrapped it around herself, shivering, gasping. "Oh, oh my! It's cold, very cold!" She tucked it over her breasts, knelt to pull out the other sheet.

Then she stopped and stared into the bucket. Taking charge, planning his day. Is that what she was doing? Selfish! William was in pain. He might just want to go home and rest. She didn't want him to go. Their drive . . . who could refuse a Lamborghini? Manipulating. Men hated that. Yet she wanted him to stay, wanted to wake up with him tomorrow morning. She'd only paid him for last night, but that was as easy as punching keys on a computer, and she hadn't made it clear that she wanted him to stay. They hadn't negotiated more. Even the words. *Negotiate. Pay.* But if she didn't, he might think her cheap. Christ! So much for her simple business transaction. She hugged her arms across her chest to stop the shivering.

"What is it, Julia?" William leaned forward.

She hesitated, looked up at him, then the words rushed out. "It's just, I was hoping you would stay with me tonight, William, but you don't have to." Stupid, of course he didn't have to. "I know we said we'd go for a drive, but I don't want you to think I'm manipulating or anything." She glanced away. "And this morning when you weren't there I was disappointed. So I want to pay you. Not for sex, or not just sex . . . Shit! Wait . . ." She held up her hand as if for a time out.

He tried not to smile, couldn't take his eyes off her. Kneeling in front of him, draped in white, a statue again, a goddess.

So much for newfound strength, Julia thought. But what he did just now in the shower . . . who would think it even possible? And those dark eyes. No wonder she was yammering; this is your brain on lust. Yet he made it seem more, as if he actually cared. Oh, he was a master! He knew exactly what women want.

Okay, strong and direct like a man. "William," she spoke deliberately, her sister's voice, the investment broker, "I'd like to pay you to stay with me until noon tomorrow. Any price you say. And I want to hear more about your clients. It's fascinating." There could not be another story like the one he'd just told. God, she hoped not. "I'll pay for that too, of course. I imagine you charge by the hour." Could run into thousands, but what the hell, find an ATM. A trip, that's all, extra expenses. Didn't come close to $489,000 for a damned hunting lodge.

She gazed down at the bucket as if she might read herbal wraps like tea leaves. "It is manipulation," she said, "isn't it? Well fine, men do it all the time, call it business." She thought a moment, then smiled up at him. "More like bait and switch, if you ask me. Courtship. Security. Oh, those are good ones too, don't you think?"

William took a moment to absorb, then leaned back and laughed. Pay him extra. Courtship, bait and switch. She was a masterpiece, all right. Like trying to follow a humming-bird. But he was up for it.

"And don't forget original sin," he said, matching her playfulness, ignoring the sarcasm. "I mean, if you think about it, that's the biggest manipulation of all, underlies everything. And only man would come up with a concept like original sin. Gotta control what you fear most."

"What?" Julia stared.

William watched her eyes brighten, as if he had pulled an exquisite gift from behind his back to surprise her. One of the job's best perks was seeing that look in women's eyes. Oh, he heard it from clients all the time. "He says I manip-ulate. Woman always manipulate." As if it were an exclusively female vice. How he loved giving them this ammunition.

It went back to that class in medieval philosophy, Dr. Snider in her orange sari telling how in the Middle Ages a woman had to be "churched" after giving birth. Had to be cleansed so she could reenter society. Had to go and kneel at the church doors and be forgiven for her sin. Birth, the most sacred gift of all, and men made it evil.

William stood, limped a step forward. No way could he get down on his knee with her, although the pain seemed better already. He looked at the ice sheet in the bucket. What the hell, might feel good.

He held out his arms. "Okay, wrap me up, baby. And pay or no pay, I'm not going anywhere, Julia. Not until you get on that plane."

Thirty-three

"So, tell me, Julia," William said later in the parking lot as he held the door for her, "what did you have to put up to rent a car like this?"

She slid in, studied her nails. "My husband's business," she said casually.

He looked at her a moment, smiled. Of course, perfect. Although she was probably kidding. And she looked perfect too, framed by the low lines of one of the world's best engineered cars. Perfect because she didn't fit at all. Midwest farm girl in a Lamborghini Murcielago. She was wearing the same yellow and white sundress with the ribbon ties. There were other choices in her suitcase, she said, but for their drive she wanted to wear this one. Okay by him. When they'd returned to the cabin he'd sat on the bed bending each hook back in place so the bodice would fasten again. It hardly seemed possible that only last night he'd ripped it open, ravished her there in the complete darkness of the tunnel.

He walked around, set their picnic lunch behind the driver's seat and the blanket Julia had found in the armoire. He got in, started the engine.

"Man. Listen to her." He shook his head, ran his hand over the dash. The day was perfect too, probably push a hundred degrees by late afternoon, but dry and clear. "Doesn't get much better, does it?" he said.

Julia smiled. "Not in my life." The clock by the CD player said 12:43.

He thought she might say more about the life she was so clearly escaping, for a weekend, anyway, but she just nestled back against the leather, luxuriating.

No, not much better, Julia thought. She'd changed his bandage when Heather brought the first-aid kit, and they lounged by the garden until their sheets were no longer cold, then went back to the room. They lay on the bed, dozed a little, naked under the skylight, like her dream. Pacing themselves for the remaining hours. She watched the number change on the clock. 12:44. This time tomorrow she'd be . . . No. Don't go there. Nothing exists but now.

"Oh, take me someplace wonderful, William," she said, turning to him. "Things I've never seen. And let's go fast. Fast enough to make everything blur."

"Well, maybe not that fast," he said. He backed the Lamborghini out, eased it into first gear. His knee was much better, only a slight twinge when he pushed in the clutch. A touch on the gas pedal, the tires spun gravel, and he let off. It'd take some getting used to. He'd never felt such power, amazing car.

The lady in the gatehouse smiled and waved as they rolled past. He stopped at the road, thought a moment. Left or right? Someplace wonderful, things she'd never seen. They could cruise Palm Springs, browse the shops and galleries, all pink stucco, nouveau Southwest. State-of-the-art mist systems cooling sidewalks and restaurant patios, crowds of tourists. No. If Julia wanted that, she would've chosen the Spa Casino or a hundred other resorts.

And suddenly he knew exactly where. "You're going to like this," he said, turning east.

Julia smiled. She would memorize everything. How big the sky was, not a single cloud, the sun glistening off the bright red hood of the Lamborghini.

William drove past the rugged slope that overlooked Hidden Springs Spa and Resort, then turned north, a gradual climb toward the distant foothills. They passed swatches of open desert and a few smaller spa hotels left over from the '60s and '70s, with their gaudy colors and low, winged roofs. Here and there a new home was under construction, right next to a vacant lot scattered with trash, old mattresses. They were on the outskirts of the town of Desert Hot Springs which was about to boom, they said. He'd believe that when he saw it. They'd have to clean out the crack houses first.

Man, this car. Just holding the wheel he could feel the shudders of restrained power. And the response, almost as if it anticipated your next move, like some machine of the future you control with your mind. He could hardly wait to get to an open stretch, let this baby go, like she wanted, but not yet.

"This area is called Miracle Hill," he said. "It's where the mineral water was first discovered. By a white man, anyway. Of course, the Indians knew long before."

"There were Indians here?"

"A thousand years, at least."

"But how could they live?" It looked so desolate to her, beautiful, but desolate. And hot. Imagine in August. Nothing but sand and rocks as far as you could see, dotted with sage brush, a few spindly trees, like the one she'd almost run into yesterday.

"They hunted and gathered," William said, "rabbits and snakes, deer higher up. Parts of the agave and yucca plants are edible, and mesquite. In spring they moved to the mountains. In the fall they moved back. The trails are still there. When I was little my grandpa used to take us arrowhead hunting on Garnet Hill," he gestured over his shoulder, "six or seven miles that way. After a rain we'd find garnets too and seashells, sometimes a fossil."

"Seashells? Out here?" she laughed. "Go on, William. Next you'll be selling me a bridge." It was more than a hundred miles to the ocean, tall mountains in between.

"It's true," he said. "Six hundred years ago this was all an inland sea." The road dead-ended at a cross street with only open desert sweeping up beyond to the hills. He stopped the car, undid his seat belt, leaned across and pointed out her window. Behind them to the southeast, they could see the whole valley below. "Over there," he said, "across on those foothills, there's a watermark thirty or forty feet up. You can follow it all along those ravines. That's how high the sea was."

She looked across the valley to the mountains, lower toward the east, ridges fingering down. She'd never seen such mountains, especially the pass she'd driven through yesterday. San Jacinto, nearly eleven thousand feet, according to the map. Ralph had a great aunt they visited once in Virginia, but the Blue Ridge was nothing compared to this.

East of the Mississippi there were no mountains, she decided, only hills.

He was leaning across her, his face close; she could smell William's hair fresh from the shower and their herbal wrap and his skin. She felt him looking at her, studying her again. She turned, met his eyes. It seemed so different out here in the open, the midday sun stripping the earth bare, not a shadow anywhere. They could be just a regular couple out for an afternoon, nothing to hide. For a moment she wondered if he might be noticing the little signs of age in her face, so close in this light, and she wanted to turn away, but then he touched her cheek, kissed her lightly, their eyes open.

What are the odds, she thought, that a simple kiss, a mere taste, a breath of him, would send pulses crackling down her sides?

Then he sat back in his seat and nodded out the windshield to the right. "Well, there it is," he said, "our first stop."

She turned, followed his eyes. "Oh, my gosh," she said, "where did that come from? I didn't even notice it."

Thirty-four

I t could have been another of her visions, a ghost building rising out of a desert hill. It was an Indian pueblo, a hodgepodge of square flat-roofed rooms built on a dozen different levels, ladders leaning against the upper walls, rustic wood beams jutting out just below the top of each box-like room. It was large, four stories high in places.

Julia half expected squaws to materialize carrying baskets of mesquite twigs, agave cuttings, papooses on their backs. Men in loincloths skinning rabbits.

Yet, it couldn't be authentic. This was not pueblo country. The Hopis were hundreds of miles away in Arizona, and as William turned the Lamborghini up the street and into the dirt parking lot, she began to see the flaws. Indians did not plaster walls with gray cement, or use glass in the windows or decorate the side yard with rusted wagon wheels and what looked like antique tools and machinery. The sign on the open gate said, CABOT'S OLD INDIAN PUEBLO MUSEUM.

"Who's Cabot?" she asked, when William came around and opened her door, helped her out.

"The guy who found the water. He homesteaded the place in 1913. Didn't build the pueblo 'til much later though. Took him twenty-three years. He died before it was finished. Come on. It's quite a story. My aunt's sister-in-law is a docent here, only reason I know about it."

He took her hand as they walked across into the side yard, shaded somewhat by a single thorny tree. Beside an old shed, its wood walls darkened with age, were pickaxes and shovels, ancient harnesses, a rusted-out wood-burning stove. Other "artifacts" were scattered around, only slightly more arranged than a junkyard. 1913. Julia thought of the photograph above the fireplace in the "Al Capone" suite, a solitary stone cabin and two gangster cars, tiny against a vast desert. That was 1930. What could've been here in 1913? Nothing.

They moved from item to item, holding hands. She listened. "This Cabot guy was born on a Lakota Sioux reservation in North Dakota," William explained, "first white baby in the county, 1880s. Parents ran the trading post there until he was five, so Cabot had an affinity for anything Indian. His mother's side was descended from John Henry Cabot, the explorer . . ."

She had been staring, seeing nothing, his words drifting by. They were standing in front of a large grinding stone, and now it blurred, her eyes filling.

"Julia?" William bent, trying to see her face. "Hey, we don't have to do this. I thought we'd just go through quickly. The inside's pretty interesting. You know, Cabot's family was from Minnesota. But let's just drive. Fine with me." He took a step toward the parking lot, still holding her hand, but she didn't budge, and when he looked back she was laughing, tears on her cheeks.

"Minnesota. Well, why didn't you say so? Of course I want to go through. We're probably related."

He laughed, relieved. Those were happy tears, at least he thought so.

Damn, she thought. Crying again, and laughing at the same time, and how could she explain? It was his hand in hers. She'd been standing there trying to remember how long it had been since she'd held hands with anyone, besides the children when they were small. What if happiness were as simple as this, seeing something together, side by side, holding hands?

She sniffed, wiped her eyes. Crazy, she'd come here to live out a fantasy, sex, that's all, and now William was giving her this too, which was almost better . . . No, what was she thinking? Not better. How could anything be better than feeling him inside her? The thought made her cheeks flush, more tears. Shit.

He ran his thumb under her eye, then the other.

In another moment she said, "William, why is it people can never seem to make it last?"

"What? You mean love?"

She nodded. She was thinking of her sister, Lucille, divorced three times, a series of relationships. And a dozen other cases she knew, even Janet Anderson, the church secretary.

William smiled, set her hand in the crook of his arm, started them toward the square archway that led around to the entrance. "Hell," he said, "if I knew the answer to that, I . . ."

A woman's loud squeal interrupted him. They stopped, looked at each other. The voice was up ahead, more squeals and yelps, and then, "What are you doing? Oh, my God. No, not here, silly! Don't. Stop it. Oh!" Laughter added to the squeals, then a man came around the corner carrying a woman over his shoulder. Her shorts had edged up showing lace panties, and she was squirming, laughing, as he spanked her bottom playfully. "Stop it, you crazy man! Put me down! Put me down!"

They were not young, was all Julia noticed at first. Silver hair, the man, anyway. The woman . . . well, you could see only her butt and legs kicking. Nice legs, but not young. Then the man turned and noticed them watching.

"Oh," he said, "ah . . . well, look who's here, honey."

That Gregory Peck voice. He swiveled a little so his captive could see. Charles Wainwright. And Helen, looking at them upside down around her husband's back now, silver hair cascading down, her eyes wide. Blushing, both of them, like kids caught doing "the nasty."

Thirty-five

Mr. Wainwright swung his wife down, helped her straighten herself, smoothing her hair, adjusting her crisp, white tennis outfit. In seconds they were completely composed, as if they'd done no more than lift the wrong fork at a dinner party, and Julia thought, that's what I want, that kind of aplomb. Clear eyed, no explanation.

"So, here we are again," Charles Wainwright said, shaking William's hand, "good to see you, son. William, isn't it? And Julia?"

"Yes." Julia smiled as he took her hand, although she did not remember telling them her name, the name she was using, anyway. Amazing that a man his age could toss his wife over his shoulder and not even appear winded.

"What happened to your head?" Charles nodded to William's bandage.

"Knocked it on the hood of my truck," William said, easily, "few stitches, that's all."

Helen Wainwright touched Julia's arm. "Isn't this place fascinating? Charles and I have been coming to Hidden Springs for years, and we've never seen this. Hardly more than a mile away. The waiter told us about it this morning, and we just walked up the road." Helen glanced up at the pueblo walls. "And wait 'til you see inside. The man was a scavenger. He took apart abandoned homestead shacks, anything he could find. Even made his own adobe."

"Really?" Julia smiled, all she could think to say. The woman had Elizabeth Taylor eyes, only warmer. Beautiful woman. Probably was in movies herself.

"You can feel the spirits," Helen was saying, "there's a kiva room inside with a dirt floor. Indians believe the earth is sacred, like a mother goddess, so when you worship, nothing can be between you and the earth." She smiled up at her husband, then at Julia. "I was telling Charles we should build one onto our house. Don't you think that's a good idea?"

The Gaia theory, Julia thought, of course the Indians

knew; the earth is a living thing. She nodded. "Yes, an excellent idea. Absolutely."

She wanted that too, the way the air seemed to change when Helen and Charles looked at each other, as if what passed between them could ionize molecules for several feet. Imagine asking Ralph to build a kiva room!

There was a silence, then Mr. Wainwright put a hand on William's shoulder, and Julia thought she noticed a slight startle in William's eyes. Charles nodded to Helen. "Honey, why don't you take Julia around to the entrance. There are a few things I'd like to say to William. You start through again, if you want. We'll catch up."

He turned to William. "That okay with you, son?"

Thirty-six

Julia hesitated, then followed Helen Wainwright through the archway. What else could she do? William gave her a nod; he seemed okay with it. Surprised, maybe, but okay. She glanced back at him as she rounded the corner. Silly, this pulled-apart feeling, like a teenager, their time too brief to waste. A few minutes, that's all.

They crossed a Santa Fe–style courtyard, the trellised walkway shaded by a vine with deep reddish purple blossoms. Bougainvillea, Julia thought. She'd seen it in movies.

A door was open at one end, and as they entered, Julia

leaned closer to Helen. "What do you think your husband wants to say to William? Is there a problem?"

Helen turned. "Problem, why would there . . . ?" She laughed. "No. Actually, Charles wants to thank him. Here, let's sit." She motioned to a bench beside a rack of faded postcards and flyers.

Julia sat beside her. They were in a small, dimly lit anteroom with dark green walls. Helen nodded toward a shadowy corner where an elderly woman with a Joan Crawford hairdo was sitting at a desk, knitting.

"She's very firm about the schedule." Helen lowered her voice to a whisper. "Like any minute there could be a flood of tourists. Charles and I were the only ones when we went through."

The woman could not be William's aunt's sister-in-law, Julia thought, unless she was much younger than she looked, or maybe he meant a great aunt. Her hair was completely white; she didn't look a day under eighty. She wasn't Hispanic or Indian, but she had the dry, wizened look of having spent entirely too much time in the sun.

"Come in, come in," the woman said then in a loud raspy voice, "have a seat. Next tour starts at one thirty."

Julia glanced at Helen. They were already sitting, and the lady hadn't even looked up, her hands still moving the needles, although the room seemed much too dark for knitting.

"She's blind." Helen mouthed the words.

Julia put her hand to her lips. She'd almost blurted out, you're kidding. A blind tour guide!

Helen nodded, whispered, "She's very good, actually. Has the place memorized."

Julia glanced around. The inside had the same disarranged feel as the yard, Indian baskets and pottery scattered on shelves, yellowed photographs on the walls, some just tacked up, not even framed.

"She memorized the photographs too?"

"Mm hmmm. They're mostly of Cabot." Helen pointed to the wall beside the shelves. "That's him with his burro and canteens. Every other day he had to trek to the railroad stop for water. Seven miles. In that next one he's digging the well."

"By hand!"

Julia jumped. It was the lady at the desk. Louder than before. She might have a Joan Crawford hairdo, but her voice was more like George Burns. Must be her tour guide voice, so the people in back could hear, or maybe she was irritated that Helen had edged in on her spiel.

"Yep, just sweat and a shovel," the lady said, same volume, her sightless eyes staring straight ahead, needles clicking. "Not like now days. 'Course he hit water at about thirty feet." Her gnarled fingers touched each stitch to check it, automatic.

Julia looked at Helen.

"Guess I got her started," Helen whispered.

"Got so hot down in the hole," the lady hollered, "he had to stand in buckets of water. Couldn't dig more than fifteen minutes at a stretch. One hundred thirty-two degrees, the water came out. Mineral water. Wasn't expecting that!" She cackled. "Afraid to drink it, he was, so he dug on the other side of the hill and got cold water. Hot and cold. Why they call this Miracle Hill." She stomped the floor. "We're on the edge of a fault right here. They say a big one is coming soon, but I wouldn't bet the farm on that. Been here eighty years myself, just a shaker now and then. 'Cept that one in ninety was sizable."

They waited, but that was it. Only her hands kept moving. Reminded Julia of the fortune teller in the glass case at the county fair when she was a girl. But the fortune-teller didn't yell. Mannequin in a head scarf. Grandpa Lawrence took her every summer, she'd pull him straight to the gypsy lady in the arcade tent, but they never told grandma. "Work of the devil," grandma would say.

Julia looked across at the old woman, silent now except the clicking of the needles. Maybe you had to put in a nickel, turn the crank, she'd start again. She felt a bit dazed, the earth could roll under her feet right now, she wouldn't be surprised. Then she remembered. She turned to Helen. "So what did William do? Why does Charles want to thank him?"

"Yes, well . . ." Helen looked at her closely, as if considering. "It happened several years ago. I'm sure you'll understand. You see, Charles thinks William saved my life."

"Saved your life?"

She nodded. "He did. I'm sure of it." In the dim light, Helen's eyes seemed a darker shade of violet. "Cancer," she said. "I'd had the surgery. They took both breasts, but it went into my lymph glands. They only gave me a few months." She shook her head, smiled. "So I made a list, things to do before I die. I guess everyone does."

Her smile turned to a grin, and she touched Julia's arm, confiding. "Only my list was more to camouflage what I really wanted. A young man, a beautiful young man. Not pretty beautiful, but more than handsome, you know what I mean?" She looked into Julia's eyes. "Yes, I'm sure you do. And the wonderful thing is, Charles agreed! Can you believe that?" She leaned back, "It still amazes me. I get this feeling, if I had done one thing differently, I wouldn't be here. And the first place I went, the Hair of the Dog on Palm Canyon Drive, there was William, sitting at the bar as if he was waiting for me. Of all the young men." She laughed. "I was wearing my turban, bald as a baby." She ran a hand over her shoulder length hair. "That was three years ago. I just had more tests Wednesday. Not a trace. We came to Hidden Springs to celebrate." She looked down. "Every day we celebrate."

Julia tried to think what to say. She'd felt a wave of something like jealousy, then it was gone. Three years. Helen might've been his first client. So if it weren't for Helen Wainwright and her breast cancer, she never would have found William that morning on her computer. Fate.

Goodness, now she was doing it, stepping into the Twilight Zone. Saved her life. That was crazy. Miracles happen, of course, especially when people believe, but doctors also make mistakes. The diagnosis could've been wrong. That was the problem with life, you never know the precise truth.

"Believe me, I've tried to understand it." Helen's voice was just above a whisper. "Maybe body chemistry can change by just deciding to live more before you die, or maybe it was that Charles understood, he loved me that much. That's plausible, isn't it? But whenever I think about it, I come back to William. It was him. I know it."

Helen stopped. She had the look of someone returning from a shrine, trying to explain, and then she said, "Something happened that night. It was like a window opened. I actually felt I would live forever, because . . ." she shrugged, "that's just how it is. He's an extraordinary young man, your William, don't you think?"

"Well . . . yes, yes he is." Julia felt herself blush. She thought of William lifting her out of the mud, carrying her, holding her in the shower. She thought of the tunnel. And how just an hour ago he'd sat on the bed, bending each hook back in place so she could wear this same dress. *Your William.* Helen thought he was her boyfriend.

"And I see the way he looks at you," Helen said, shaking her head. "You can't imagine what women would give for that look."

A thousand dollars, Julia thought, smiling, but she didn't say it.

Helen touched her arm. "And how long have you known him, honey?"

Julia laughed. "What time is it?"

"One twenty-seven," the blind woman shouted, "three minutes. Tour starts at one thirty prompt. Best go on out and tell your men."

Julia and Helen looked at each other.

"Well," Julia said, "in three minutes I will have known William exactly, let's see . . . nineteen and a half hours."

Helen studied her with those violet eyes. "No, that's impossible. I can't believe that. You must've known him in another life."

Thirty-seven

"So, ladies . . ." In the doorway, Charles Wainwright took a moment to adjust from the bright sunlight, then walked to them, lifted Helen to her feet.

William followed, and Julia sensed immediately something was different. He smiled, but he seemed . . . distracted, almost troubled. He came and took her hand. "How're you doing?"

She nodded. "Fine . . . and you?" But he didn't answer, and before she could say more, the old woman stepped from behind her desk.

"Welcome! Welcome to Cabot's Old Indian Pueblo," she

called out. "Right this way, ladies and gentlemen. Stay together, now."

There was nothing to do but follow her through the odd structure and listen as she yelled her explanations. A hodgepodge of rooms tacked on over the years to no particular plan, except whatever materials Cabot scavenged at the time. A wall paneled with wood from an old printing press; you could stand and read the news, backwards, 1927. The cubicle Cabot carved from the hillside when he first arrived, so he could sleep without worrying about rattlesnakes. And everywhere Indian artifacts, dream catchers, a full Sioux headpiece, totems from Cabot's time with the Inuits. Most amazing to Julia was how the old lady negotiated every turn, stepping up and down through uneven doorways, not even a cane to tap her way.

Julia tried to read William's eyes, but his face was blank, faraway, and she found no opportunity to ask. The woman hardly paused, and if they tried the slightest whisper she'd *shush* them. Old schoolteacher, probably. What was William thinking? Julia wondered. Had she said something wrong? Or was he just feeling the same frustration of having their time usurped, first the Wainwrights and now the blind Tour Nazi.

When at last they exited onto the dirt courtyard, the old woman touched Julia's arm. "One more thing, over here. You'll especially like this, honey."

She led them to a large grinding stone set on a pedestal about waist high. Carved in the center was a peephole that pointed up toward the distant mountains. "Look through there," the old woman said, nodding, "Tahquitz, the rascal god." She pointed toward the tallest peak. "The rocks form an angel," she cackled, "or a big white bird. Indians say Tahquitz would come down and steal chickens, or a woman sometimes." She gave Julia a nudge. "Go on, look." Julia bent, peered through the hole. "Stole the chief's wife once. They found her up in the canyons by a pool, but when they brought her back, she just ran off again. That's the legend, anyway."

"Yes, there. I see. Wings. It's very clear." Julia stood back for William. She was about to whisper something about the rascal god stealing women, but he shook his head.

"I've seen it before," he said, flatly, "and we'd better be going."

Thirty-eight

They watched the old lady make her way back across the courtyard to the little anteroom where they'd started. Amazing, Julia thought, counting steps, probably. Tahquitz god.

They said their good-byes and waved as the Wainwrights started down the hill, arm in arm. "You two have fun," Helen called.

"Maybe we'll see you at dinner," Charles added.

"William," Julia said, turning, "is something wr . . . ?" But he was already paces ahead, on his way to the parking lot in the other direction. She caught up. "Helen told me about her cancer, William, and what happened. She was your first client, wasn't she?"

He stopped. "Yes. Why?"

Something was wrong. She could hear it in his voice. "Nothing," she said. "It's interesting, that's all, but . . . you seem different. What's wrong? Did Charles say something . . ."

"No. Or not intentionally . . ." He saw her wince, tried to soften his voice. "Look, Julia, it's just . . . it's not supposed to be like this. You're not supposed to ask about other clients, much less meet one, sit and compare notes . . ."

"We didn't compare notes." She looked away.

"I know, I'm sorry. I didn't mean that, but the whole thing doesn't work if . . . well, there has to be a kind of . . . integrity."

"Integrity?"

She managed not to smile. He had snapped at her. He didn't have to snap at her.

"Yes, integrity, damn it. Like getting out of character in the middle of a play. You have to accept the premise that it isn't real. You can't go asking each other a lot of questions, as if you're a . . ." William wiped his brow. He'd almost said "couple." Standing in the sun, sweat beading his forehead, dripping under the bandage. He gave a laugh. "The man thanks me for saving his wife's life. Jesus! I fucked her. Her mind did the rest. So I'm good. Not exactly something to put on a resumé."

She listened. What could she say?

He nodded toward the parking lot. "Look, Julia, it's hot out here. Right now I just want to drive, is that okay?" He started walking again.

"Of course, but you could at least . . . wait for me." Shit, her tone said more: I am paying for you, you know. *And* the damn car. He didn't have to snap at her.

William turned back, took her hand. They continued to the parking lot. He opened her door. She got in. He walked around. He drove without speaking, east, away from Hidden Springs.

And Julia thought, what the hell is this? If she wanted a fight and the ensuing silence, she could've stayed home. Although lately she and Ralph skipped right to the silence. Or she could be back in the grotto, soaking up minerals . . . by herself. A hovering feeling went through her chest, like leaning over a cliff. What could Charles Wainwright have said that would change everything, steal these last hours from them?

No, she thought, do not overreact. This wasn't like William. He would explain, once he calmed down. Right, like she knew him so well, twenty-some hours. Already making excuses for him.

The road ran through open desert now, parallel to the

foothills, and she could see the washes fanning down, piles of boulders here and there, clumps of snarled branches, uprooted trees.

"Flash floods," William said, and she waited, but that was all.

Why wouldn't he talk to her? Well, he had to concentrate on driving, of course. With each wash there was a dip in the road, some only a half mile apart. He was taking the Lamborghini as fast as he could on the open stretches and still manage to slow for the next dip. "Tummy tumblers," her kids called them. When they'd hit the first one, she felt the wheels leave the pavement. She let out a whoop, couldn't help it. "Yes!"

But he was more careful after that. "I'm no Evel Knievel," he said.

In maybe fifteen miles they turned off into a parking lot, a large clump of shaggy palm trees at the far end. THOUSAND PALMS OASIS, the sign said. He turned the key, the engine shuddered down.

"What a car!" he said. "Thanks, Julia."

"You're welcome."

He turned to her. "So, how 'bout that picnic? You hungry?"

"Famished!" She managed a smile. He seemed better.

William reached for the door, then stopped. "They think you're my girlfriend."

"I know."

His eyes softened more. "He said how beautiful you are."

She felt a blush start, but she could see something was still troubling him.

He looked past her. "Wainwright. Christ, thanking me for saving her life! It's just, I thought they knew about my 'career.'" He gestured quote marks in the air, his tone mocking. "But why would they? That time with Helen could've been just once, a fluke. Should've been." He looked down. "A man like that. I felt . . . I mean, the guy's so dignified, successful, and that resemblance. It's like talking to a ghost. I felt like a kid, a dumb shit."

William stopped. How he sounded, but this whole damned weekend was insane. Nancy Carlton, Erma Smedley. Wainwright shaking his hand, thanking him. And worst, Julia making him feel again, making him think.

Julia touched his arm. She wanted to hold him. You're young, she'd say. You can do anything you want. But she stayed quiet.

He met her eyes. "He asked what I do for a living. Fuck!"

She put her hand to her mouth, tried not to laugh.

Then he realized and laughed, shaking his head. "Ooh, boy. I lied, of course. Said I was in grad school."

Thirty-nine

"Evil results from the failure of rationality."

"What?"

"'Evil results from the failure of rationality.' Hannah Arendt." William stared up at the sky, musing. "I've been thinking about that all morning."

They were lying flat on their backs in the palm oasis, lounging peacefully, digesting their sliced turkey breast on croissants. From the road, they had hiked a mile-long trail winding through low dunes to the largest grove. A warm breeze rustled the fat bearded palms that shaded them from the afternoon sun.

Ah, yes, Julia thought. Their mud bath conversation, brought on by the woman who'd split William's head open this morning in some sleazy motel room. She preferred not to be reminded.

"I really liked that class," William said. Grad school. Maybe he would start again next semester, at least a class or two.

Julia looked at him. He seemed far away again, like someone glancing up from a book, yet still immersed in it.

". . . failure of rationality," he repeated, his voice shifting. "But how the hell are we supposed to know what's rational?"

Julia laughed. "How indeed?"

She wished they'd never stopped at that crazy pueblo, never seen the Wainwrights. She wanted William back, the way it was before, when they were strangers. He was right about not asking too many questions, not trying to make it real. As soon as you know too much about the person, as soon as you take off the mask, the fantasy dissolves. Absorbed now in his philosophies. She wanted him to pay attention to her. She wanted what she had paid for, damn it! But she couldn't say that. Ruin everything. If it wasn't already ruined. The dry grass felt prickly through the blanket, and she squirmed to get more comfortable.

This place didn't help. Wild and unkempt, almost eerie. So quiet. Only an occasional frog chirruping in the pond. A pond, way out here! Huge shaggy palms, several hundred years old, William had said, some with trunks charred and black all the way to the top, yet still alive. A jungle of dried fronds piled against the hollow husks of fallen trees. Tall reeds along the water's edge, salt patches seeping up. A compilation of plant smells, heat on the water, the sweet musk of decay. To her, it could have been another planet. The hush seemed as thick as the moist and dusty air, as if one could hardly breathe and speak at the same time.

She wanted the time they had left, that's all. She could feel it ticking away, the sun blinking through the palm fronds. Three o'clock, edging towards four. Maybe when they were back at Hidden Springs time would slow again. If she could stop time completely, if this were the last day of her life, would she care? No, not a whit. No ending could be better. And the next weeks and months and years . . .

Not yet, she thought. Not yet.

She turned to William. *Evil results from the failure of rationality*. Think. Say something intelligent, philosophic. Bring him back to her.

"Maybe it has to do with definitions," Julia said in another moment. "Or . . . perspective."

"Hmm?" William opened his eyes. He'd been considering what else Charles Wainwright had said and whether to tell Julia. But what was the point of telling her? *Well, if grad school doesn't work out, I might have a job for you.* No, the old guy was probably just blowing smoke, vacation talk that dissolves Monday morning. He'd heard plenty of that. Besides, Wainwright had the wrong idea entirely. *Beautiful girl,* he'd said, *and she's in love with you, son. Clear as the nose on your face. Not something to take lightly either.*

Why wouldn't grad school work out, if he really set his mind to it?

William smiled. Funny old couple. Still living in the '40s. Nice, but way out there. Well, the world was not Fred Astaire and Ginger Rogers anymore. And Julia was not his girlfriend. She was a client, and in less than twenty hours she would be gone.

William turned toward her on the blanket, propped on an elbow, shaded his eyes from the sun. He didn't know which was better, the way her face lit up with laughter or this, so serious, watching him. Either way, he wanted to take her in his arms. He was getting hard again. So much for his illustrious talent, hard-on-at-will and only at will. Except that brief lapse with Nancy Carlton.

"I'm sorry, Julia," he said. "What did you just say?"

Forty

"Well," Julia took a breath, "I was thinking about what you said, how we know what's rational. Don't you think it depends on definitions and . . . perspective? Maybe our definitions are too narrow, too literal . . ." She paused. "No, linear. Linear is a better word."

"What do you mean?" He leaned closer.

Julia smiled. He was interested again, pleased. She wanted to please him, but she wasn't sure she could put it into words. Maybe if she backed up to the beginning and didn't look at his eyes.

"Okay." She focused past him to the base of a palm tree. "Like that Cabot guy. I mean, most people would think he was just a crackpot. Didn't choose Palm Springs because there were too many people." She laughed. "Nineteen thirteen. Couldn't have been more than a dozen families. Feeding the damn rattlesnakes so they'd hang around as watch dogs. Goodness! The place is a monstrosity. A wonder they didn't just tear it down when he died."

"They almost did," William said. "Lots of old buildings around here were only spared because of the slump of the eighties. Especially in Palm Springs. By the time the economy revived, they were considered quaint." He laughed. "But you're right, Cabot was way beyond quaint."

Where was she going with all this? Julia's mind was like a dance. Maybe he'd get a credential, take a job at the high school, then go find her in Minnesota. In a year. Right. What were the odds? Is that how people settled into jobs they hated? "Lives of quiet desperation"? Or maybe a quiet life was just what he needed.

"But it was all because of the Indians, if you think about it," Julia went on, "that's what I mean about perspective. If Cabot hadn't live with the Indians when he was little, then later in Alaska. Fifteen years old, the lady said, when he went off to the Gold Rush." She shook her head. "Made a fortune selling cigars to the miners, met Teddy Roosevelt. My God, it could be a movie. Lived with the Inuits, translated their language. Indians. That's what made him so odd, to us anyway."

Excited now, she moved to her knees, hiked up her skirt, sat cross-legged on the blanket facing him. "See what I mean?" she said. "A whole different perspective."

Oh, he saw, all right. She wasn't wearing any panties. That lovely dark blond patch . . . William forced his eyes back up to her face. She hadn't seemed to notice. Went right on building her logic, cheeks flushed.

"And that kitchen," she said, "windows and doors all skewed, because Indians believe straight lines hold in the evil spirits. Everything has to be slightly crooked so they can get out." She laughed. "Evil spirits, to us that just sounds crazy, like a kiva room with a dirt floor because the earth is sacred. But most indigenous people believe that sort of thing. While we want the world to be linear, symmetrical, all neat and straight and 'modern.' We wouldn't even call their ideas rational. What would we call them? We'd call them . . ."

"Uncivilized," William said. "Yes. Or primitive." God, he wanted her. He wanted to listen and devour her at the same time. The biggest sex organ, after all, is the brain. He glanced again, couldn't help it.

"Exactly," she said. "Uncivilized. What a license that is. Like the whole idea of progress. Indians probably didn't even have a concept of progr . . ." She stopped. She'd been using the word *Indian* and *we*, meaning white. But William was mostly Indian, Aztec or something, those dark eyes and skin. Still, she didn't think he was offended. No, not the way he was looking at her. She followed his eyes, pulled her skirt down, blushing.

William edged closer, but she held her hand against his chest.

"Wait, there's more. I'm getting there. If I can just think . . ." She could feel his skin warm beneath her hand, and her fingers closed on his shirt, pulled him to her. "Oh, never mind, never mind . . ."

He kissed her hard, quick, hungry kisses, her lips, her neck, her eyes. "No, don't stop," he said, "Progress. 'Man's ability to complicate simplicity.' I forget who said that, but go on, Julia. I want to hear. Really." He smiled. "Turns me on. You can't imagine." He pulled the ribbon ties on her shoulders, kissed her breasts, leaned her back on the blanket, working the hooks and eyes, slipping off her sundress, then his shirt, his jeans. "Go ahead, talk to me, Julia. Tell me."

She gasped as he moved down. My God, he wanted her to talk philosophy. It turned him on. She laughed. "I was wondering when we were going to get kinky."

He laughed too, but didn't stop kissing. Ah yes, delicious journey, gentle slope, rib cage to waist, knoll and valley, his favorite little glen just below the hipbone. And down.

Okay, she thought, breathing in, I can do this, I can. Concentrate. Oh, my God! "It's just . . . to know what's rational . . . we . . . we'd have to see the whole picture . . . Oh, God, like that, yes . . . We'd have to see the way people think . . . everywhere . . . we'd have to understand every culture, every religion . . . every philosophy . . . Oh, sweet Jesus!" She arched as he lifted her hips, flicked his tongue.

"Go on, don't stop," he murmured.

"And . . . oh my . . . it's . . . it's impossible to understand all that. Only God can see everything. So . . . the closest we can get is . . . love."

"Love?" He stopped, looked up at her.

She nodded. How beautiful he was, there against her Minnesota white skin. In a moment he would enter her and time would stand still.

"Yes," she said, "love." Their eyes held a moment, then she went on. "Because love is how we know God. Love transcends rational thinking, wouldn't you say? Love may even be the ultimate rationality because . . . it isn't tied to any language or culture or rule, yet it works. Like quantum physics. So of course 'evil results from a failure of rationality . . .'"

She looked past him as he reached into his pocket. Then she pulled him up onto her, felt him ease in, gasped. She moved against him, slowly, slowly, whispering now, smiling.

"So, Mr. Professor, what do you think your Hannah Arendt would say about that?"

Forty-one

They lay holding each other, getting their breath, the dusty palms standing guard around them. And William knew he could not go with her to the airport tomorrow. No way could he see her walk onto a plane.

He eased to one side so he wasn't too heavy on her, then lay quiet, listening to her breathe. Her eyes were closed. She was smiling. How could he let her go? He would call Charles Wainwright. If Wainwright meant what he'd said . . . "Hollywood, bit parts at first, then who knows, with your looks." The studio was in Baja, Mexico, just past Rosarito Beach, better than Hollywood, actually, as far as

William was concerned. He had no interest in Hollywood, already knew about living off your looks. He wanted more than that. Still, he had to do something. His cell phone was in the car. Damn. He wanted to get up, go call Wainwright now, but he knew better. Give her time.

Minutes passed. Her breathing slowed, her eyes fluttered under closed lids, then her body jerked suddenly and she looked up at him. "Oh," she said, her voice groggy, "was I asleep? I don't want to sleep. Don't let me sleep. Tonight we'll drink coffee, lots of coffee . . ."

She drifted off, and William thought how little he knew of her life at home. He wanted to ask. Better not. Leave what was left of her fantasy.

In moments she woke again, met his eyes. He had been watching her sleep, and in his look was such tenderness . . . She felt her cheeks redden, nestled against his chest, breathed his skin. This is enough, she thought, lying here naked in the shade of these silent palms, the desert sky a perfect blue. She could die now. The earth could open and swallow them, no tomorrow.

She listened for some subterranean shifting beneath them, almost willed it, right here, one of the world's largest earthquake faults. It could happen. No better moment. One should be able to choose, she thought. Like Thelma and Louise. A last bright flash that redefines the rest. But she heard only his heartbeat, and then, not far away, a birdcall of some kind.

"Quail," William whispered. "Look, there."

She turned to see a family scurry across a low dune to the edge of the grass not ten feet away. Like partridges only smaller, the half-grown young following in a straight line. The male with his curved plume leading the way. One by one they disappeared into the skirt of a fan palm.

William's lips brushed below her ear, and she closed her eyes. Whatever happened now was extra, she thought, a gift. It was all a gift. Nothing could take it. Death was just a painted face, miming to an empty street. She had come all this way. It was enough.

Fronds shifted above, and she looked up at the glinting sun. It had hardly moved in the sky. Maybe twenty minutes had passed, no more. Silly thoughts, earthquakes, death. William's chest was warm against her back. There were hours left. Hours she would not trade for anything.

Forty-two

They walked the trail back to the car, and as Julia settled into the passenger seat, William leaned across, retrieved his cell phone from the console. On his way around he dialed Charles Wainwright. No answer, only voice mail. He left a message, got in, started the engine. "It's not quite five o'clock," he said, "shall we drive a little more?"

Julia nodded. "I'd like that." She wondered who he had called. Checking appointments? But she would not ask. What did she expect? Still, she felt a slight catch below her ribs, disappointment. He could've waited until she was gone.

She pushed it aside. No, don't ruin it. Live in the moment. She leaned against the soft leather. It felt good after lying on the ground. There was still a raw place on her back from last night, the dirt wall of the tunnel. And other soreness. She smiled.

They took the back road east to the I-10, then up the long, steep grade sprinkled with RVs hauling boats and jet skis and dirt bikes for playgrounds on the Colorado River. The Lamborghini veered in and out easily. People stared and pointed, and more than one semi blasted its air horn.

Julia waved, her sense of urgency all but gone. It didn't matter how far they went, how long it took to get back. Sun roof open, basking in this absolute luxury. They could keep right on going, cross the continent for all she cared, but in minutes William took the cutoff north to the high desert. He slowed some on the narrower road, and she watched the landscape change, content with this too, and the delicious surge of power as he accelerated out of the curves.

"Man, this car!" William said. Solid, not a centimeter of play in the wheel, like holding the whole machine in your grasp. He recited the names of desert plants for her, the ones he knew. Tall ocotillos and yuccas with their fading blooms, beavertail and prickly pear. He pointed out entire hillsides of jumping cholla, like advancing armies. "You should see it in spring," he said, "after a rain there are wild flowers everywhere." He nodded out the windshield, "purple verbena, daisies, desert poppies. The ocotillos have bright red tips like candles. Even the cactus bloom."

"Goodness," she said, "I thought desert was just desert. What are those, there?"

"Joshua trees. Not actually trees," he added, "they're in the yucca family. They have a flower like a lily."

They wound higher, across a rolling plain studded with these odd "trees," thirty feet tall some of them, with clumps of spiny leaves. Amazing, Julia thought, that such a scruffy looking "tree" could blossom like a lily.

When the road straightened William eased the pedal down. Instant response. Lamborghini Murcielago, like some vehicle of the future you drive simply by thinking. Ninety, one hundred, didn't touch what this baby could do. The tires squealed as they took a wide curve, and he braked just enough. Julia was quiet, gazing out her window.

Seeing this for the first time, William thought, must be something, compared to Minnesota. Ten thousand lakes. He tried to imagine all that green, then the winters. He never even saw snow up close 'til he was twelve. There was so much he wanted to ask her. He wanted to know how her life was growing up, what dreams she'd had, how she met her husband, how old her children were. Mostly, he wanted to ask about her marriage. The women he'd known these last few years, clients, were unhappily married, but then they weren't exactly a cross section. You couldn't base a study on them.

How many really good marriages did he know? Half his cousins were divorced, aunts and uncles too. Grandma Estella had been happy, but that was a different generation. Still, just because Julia wanted this adventure, didn't mean she wanted out of her marriage.

The next moment they spoke at once.

"Could I ask you someth . . . ?"

"So, William, will you tell me . . ."

They laughed.

"Go on," he said, "you first."

"It's just, well, I thought you might tell me some of your stories," she said, "you know, from your work."

He glanced across at her, then back at the road. "Mmm, I'm not sure . . ."

"Oh, I don't want to break your rule . . . well, maybe bend it a little. But I'm so curious. When I think of the perspective you must have about women, about life, human nature. My God, how rare is that?"

He didn't answer. Stories from his "work." It felt like standing on the edge of a minefield. Surprising, though, that no client had ever asked, much less put it in those terms. He glanced at Julia again. No, not surprising. This morning crying in his arms, now eager to know more.

Her expression brightened with a sudden idea and she leaned closer, touched his arm. "I know," she said, "we could make it a road game, like finding the alphabet on billboards or Twenty Questions."

He could feel the energy in her fingertips. Her eyes playful, seducing him now. What wouldn't he do for this woman? *Minefield.*

"My kids call it the Animal, Vegetable or Mineral game," she said. "Did you ever play Twenty Questions on a trip?"

He laughed. "Once with my nieces and nephews. We didn't do a whole lot of traveling when I was a kid." Animal, vegetable, mineral. He could categorize clients that way. Nancy Carlton, mineral. Erma Smedley, vegetable *and* animal. The road wound higher.

"So," he said, "does that mean I get to just answer yes or no?"

"Hmm." She thought a moment. "We could try it. I'll do three test questions, okay? These don't count. Ready?"

"Ready."

She took a breath. "What do most of your clients ask fo . . . ? No, wait, that won't work. Yes or no." She reworded. "Has anyone ever asked for something you wouldn't do?"

He held up one finger, counting.

"Yes."

Her voice lifted, surprised. "Really? What?"

She leaned forward, trying to read his eyes, but he kept them steady on the road, held up two more fingers.

"I believe that's three questions," he said calmly. "You sure that's what you want to ask?"

It took a moment to sink in. "Get outta here, William! You can't do that!" She punched his arm, laughing.

He slowed the Lamborghini, pulled to the side of the road, careful not to go off into the soft sand. Still chuckling, he pushed the lever, the doors swung up, and the cooler air of the high desert washed over them. He went around, took her hands. He was buying time. And if they were entering dangerous territory he wanted to be able to hold her, in case of shrapnel.

"Come on," he said, "let's walk a little. I'll tell you what I can. It's a career I'm winding down anyway."

Forty-three

They stood on a vast plateau under a vaulted blue sky. There was no sound. Even the wind was silent, as if the slightest rustle were swallowed by the immense dome. It almost felt like talking in church, congregation of Joshua trees and brittlebush, the occasional boulder.

He started with her question (Has anyone ever asked for something you wouldn't do?) and told the story of his shortest appointment ever. Should've figured by the address, a condo complex in south Palm Springs. But as soon as the door opened, he knew. She was not a she. Although William had to say the makeup and wig were damned good. It was the stance, the tilt of the head, a tad exaggerated, more woman than a woman. And the hands, there's little you can do about the hands.

"I left," he said, and Julia nodded, her hand to her mouth.

When he didn't tell her was how the guy grabbed his arm as he turned to go. *Come on, whore, a gig's a gig. You'll like it.* A deep baritone, in his other hand something black, a harness. William knew he was not at all homophobic, but still he flattened the guy with a quick punch. Whore.

At least the story gave him time to weed through some that were easier to tell. If he had to pick his most typical client, he supposed it would be Nancy Carlton. Rich wives still living in the '50s. Each with her own quirks. Marking time between dinner parties and redecorating and wondering where the husband is. Women who think fulfillment is a credit card with no limit, who spend their whole lives behind gates and think they're free.

"A lot of it isn't what you might imagine," William said then. "With my fee I could see three or four clients a month and get by, except I've been building a nest egg, and, well, it gets addictive, the money not the . . . sex." His voice had dropped to a whisper. What was that about? Why was this difficult, what was the risk? Hearing it himself, probably.

He took a breath. "Women do hire me as just an escort, you know."

"Right," Julia said, laughing.

"It's true. One lady a couple years ago. She was a widow, very rich, about sixty, I think. Hard to tell with the work they all get now."

"Work?"

William smiled. "Plastic surgery, you know, face lifts, Botox, lipo." Minnesota, he thought, where a peel still has to do with fruit. Maybe it was time to relocate, anywhere but Southern California.

"She had me take her to all her society functions," he went on, "the limo, the tux, the whole nine yards. Interviewed me first to be sure I could pass, wouldn't sound like a wetback gardener." He grinned. "For once my philosophy major paid off. We went to all these fancy receptions, balls, galas. She introduced me as her boyfriend. She loved it, making her friends jealous. 'He doesn't even golf,' she'd say, 'can you believe?' Then she'd whisper about other ways we found to stay fit. But we never had sex, never even kissed. It went on for over a year 'til she met a man on a cruise and remarried." He laughed. "She paid me to go to the wedding and look sad."

"Oh, my gosh." Julia laughed. She hardly thought it could be true, although it seemed too elaborate to make up. The way he looked now, the sun over his shoulder, all that blue sky. How handsome in a tuxedo, what woman could resist?

"So," she said, "tell me what most women wanted. Normal women."

"Well, I don't know if I could say *most*. They're all . . . different." Shit, watching her, careful. He felt like one of those army engineers scanning for tiny detonators, lying on his belly, sweating over which wire to cut. "Or . . . I guess it's the same as what men want, what they don't get at home, the married ones, anyway . . . oral sex and someone to listen." His voice lowered again, automatic, although there probably wasn't another human being for miles.

"Yes," she said, "I could see that. What else?"

So far so good. He took her hand, headed them toward a clump of rocks some fifty yards away. "All right. Some come to me because, well, they have trouble having orgasms . . . during sex, that is. For women it's mental, has to do with relaxation techniques, like yoga, meditation. I have some methods." He grinned. "Things it's safe to try at home."

"Yes. I know." She nodded. "Oh, do I know." She imagined dozens of women breathing deeply, conjuring up William. Husbands wondering what brought this on. A new *Cosmo* article probably. Is that what she would do . . . for the rest of her life?

"I figure it worked if they didn't come back," he said. "Most didn't."

They stepped around a large dead "tree," spiny branches strewn around the corpse. "Careful, they'll go right through your sandals." His hand on her back.

They were quiet a few moments, savoring the cool wind. How many had there been? Julia wondered. But she only said, "Go on, William."

He stifled a sigh. "Well, some, quite a few, actually, came to me out of revenge, the husband having an affair." He watched closely, a clue to her own motivation, perhaps, but she didn't look up. "And for some it was just a lark, like a bachelor party thing or a dare."

She stopped walking, her eyes widened. "You do parties, William?"

"No. No, of course not. I meant like a once-in-a-lifetime . . . a celebratory thing." He would not tell about the twins who hired him for their thirty-fifth birthday, a gift to each other. Frozen dessert heiresses they were, Sara Lee or something, in a lull between husbands. Private jet, a penthouse suite at the Bellagio. Twins, every man's dream, except halfway through they started arguing like teenagers, and he ended the evening in a taxi to the airport. No problem, five thousand dollars in his pocket. Vegas. They could've hired three or four guys, but then there would've been nothing to fight about.

Shit, where did he get off thinking smack about rich women and their empty lives? What about his life? Where was his fucking fulfillment? Three years wasted, telling himself he was doing a fucking study. Literally, oh yeah, he heard it, but it wasn't funny. He had lost Linda because of it. Even now if he got out and managed to build a normal life, his past would always be there, like a tumor too dangerous to remove . . . He stopped the thought. More bullshit. A male "escort" was just quaint, a boy toy. If you want to talk risk, try counting the bodies of hookers they found now and then in shallow graves outside Vegas. None were male, that's sure.

He glanced at Julia. She was watching the ground as they walked, stepping carefully. They skirted a patch of cholla skeletons, covered with tiny barbed needles as fine as fur. If he had gloves he could show her how to peel the dried skin and barbs, the wood smooth and hollow underneath, perforated in rows. A handful of mesquite seeds inside, they made perfect rain sticks. He and his cousins used to sell them to tourist shops. He scanned the gnarled branches for a straight one. Maybe make her a rain stick to take home . . . Crazy. Hardly a trip for souvenirs. Her family probably didn't even know where she was.

They reached the rocks and found two that were suitable for sitting. When he released her hand, Julia felt how moist his palm was, saw the strain in his eyes. Not a good idea, making him tiptoe like this around the truth. She looked past him, back toward the road.

"I'm sorry, William, I shouldn't have asked . . . Oh, my gosh, look at those boulders!" In the distance the Joshua tree forest gave way to huge rock formations. She stood, shaded her eyes from the sun. Massive rocks, some as big as houses, balanced one on top of another. "It seems so deliberate and yet unreal." She pointed. "Look, look at that one, like Noah's ark after the flood. I've never seen anything like it." She turned. "Oh, we have to go there. I want to see them closer."

William smiled. It was why he'd brought her here. And she could not have missed them before. She was letting him off the hook. He'd made it through.

When they reached the car, he suggested she might want to drive, but she preferred to stay glued to the window. The road continued to climb, winding through the formations. Near the top they pulled into a view point and they got out. He took her hand and they walked the short path to a platform jutting out over a point, three-hundred-and-sixty-degree view, miles and miles. The wind blew harder up here, whipping at her dress, and he stood sheltering her. She leaned against his chest. The elevation was over four thousand feet, twenty degrees cooler. To the north they could see the road they'd driven and the sweep of high desert with those piles of huge boulders.

"It's like giants gathered them for rock fights," Julia said. "I can just see them thundering around, hiding behind their piles."

"Mmm." William nodded.

They turned and crossed the platform, Julia holding her skirt against the gusts, shivering. The point looked out over the entire Coachella Valley, the sky just starting to soften into sunset. William stood behind, rubbed her arms. "That's the Salton Sea," he said, pointing to the southeast, "forty miles long, and from here it looks like a puddle. With good binoculars we could see Mexico." Across were the peaks of the Santa Rosas, a haze of smog hovering in the western pass.

He couldn't stand it, he had to ask. He turned her to him, took her hands, the wind blowing her hair. "Julia," he said, "before, what I started to ask. There's something I need to know. Will you be okay when you go back home?"

But as soon as the words were out, he saw his mistake. Of course, when you least expect. A land mine after all.

Forty-four

She stared at him, and he could see the struggle behind her eyes, that tightening to keep from crying. Her lips formed the word, *okay*, but the sound was taken by the wind, and in that moment William noticed she was perhaps older than he'd thought. He didn't care. Forty-two, forty-three? Made no difference. Julia was the most beautiful woman he'd ever known.

She took her hands from his, folded her arms across her chest, looked away. Her body shuddered as she drew a deep breath, chewed her lip.

William tried to think what words could erase what he had said. Damn fool! Couldn't just let it be, these last hours before she walked onto that plane. He wanted to take her in his arms, but was afraid she'd push him away. He waited, helpless.

Okay, Julia thought, squinting up at the sky, arms tight across her chest, eyes burning, angry. *Okay*. Stupid, stupid word! Twenty years it had been her mantra. It's okay. You have a nice home. He pays the bills. He doesn't beat you. Nothing's perfect. It's just the way he is. And the years stretch on. And suddenly the kids are raised, and you're forty-six fucking years old! Too late for anything but one crazy weekend. A fantasy, that's all.

She closed her eyes. She'd been about to say, And you? Will you be okay? Sarcastic. Checking his damn appointments! Shaping his stories to protect her, patronizing . . . No, not that. Her anger had nothing to do with William. Just an innocent question. He couldn't know. It was the whole damned setup, wheels in motion, and how easy it is to forget to live. As if death weren't long enough so you had to start early. Stupid!

She was shaking. Cold, so cold up here. And suddenly she heard the silliness. Like a slap. What was she thinking? She was from Minnesota, don't ya know. This wasn't cold. Not even close.

She ran her hands through her hair, wild and tangled, stretched her arms into the wind. There was no time now for anger or tears. Like that almost argument they'd had after the pueblo. William had things to work out in his own life, but that was later, not now. If she let this steal the time remaining, it'd be her own stupid fault. Shooting herself in the foot.

She turned back to him, her eyes softening some. She would have this night with him. In that antique bed under the stained glass lily pads. Oh, she'd had years of practice turning these corners in her mind, avoiding ugliness, appeasing, crab-walking around the slightest snag, the slightest confrontation.

But this, this time was for herself.

She smiled. "You know what, William, I'm really hungry," she said. "Could we just go find someplace to eat?"

Forty-five

I t's the smile, William thought, like breathing pure oxygen, feeling your cells renew. Continents explored, masterpieces created, empires built, all for a woman's smile.

"I know the perfect place," he said, "it's back down the hill." He took her hand. "Come on, we'll find out just what the Murcielago can do."

They circled west down highway 62 through Yucca Valley and the Morongo Pass, chasing the sunset, slowing on the curves only enough to keep all four wheels on the road. Julia gripped the bars beside her seat, let out a whoop with each adrenaline surge, watched the rearview mirror for cops.

"Thirty-six minutes all the way from the view point to Desert Hot Springs," William said, "gotta be a record." He pulled into the restaurant parking lot, spinning gravel. "So, do you like Mexican food, Julia?"

She laughed, splaying her fingers, her knuckles coloring again. "I've never tried it."

William looked at her. "Go on, you're kidding."

"Well, a taco once at a food court in the Mall of Americas, if that counts."

He laughed, pulled the lever and the Lamborghini's doors swung up, like bat wings. A couple coming out of the restaurant stared. One of the best features, these doors, like stepping from a landing craft. The couple whispered to each other as William walked around to Julia's portal. Thought they were celebrities, probably. He waited while Julia smoothed her hair, worked the tangles out with her fingers.

Not bad, she thought, checking the mirror. The Goldie Hawn look, Melanie Griffith.

SOUTH OF THE BORDER, the sign said. Like a hacienda, whitewashed outer wall, an arch with an iron bell, heavy rabbeted doors. They crossed a small courtyard thick with bougainvillea and hibiscus, a fountain made of copper pots and blue tile, birdcages hung from porch beams. Julia stood on tiptoes, made whistling and kissing sounds, and the birds chirped back.

"My grandma always has songbirds." William smiled. "It's a Mexican thing."

Julia looked up, listened. Music was coming from inside, music that made hips and shoulders move automatically. To think she'd almost suggested they go back to Hidden Springs, eat at the restaurant there. Guitar and maracas, a trumpet. Oh, this was wonderful!

"William," she said, "what's that drink they have? The one with the worm?"

"Tequila." He laughed, holding the door for her. "You want tequila?"

"Yes, oh, yes!" She slid by, touched his cheek. "But don't let me drink too much. I am not sleeping tonight."

The walls inside were decorated with bright Mexican serapes and sombreros, bullfight posters and Aztec paintings, and here and there were bouquets of huge paper flowers, yellow and fuchsia and bright blue, amid wrought-iron lamps and ropes of red peppers hanging by the bar. The booths were dark wood, scrolled and carved, a row of tables in the center. The restaurant was only half full, and she noticed several women look up at William. Of course.

They followed a waiter to a corner booth, ordered margaritas. "I love this," Julia said, "it's like the movies. The world should have more color, don't you think?"

"Absolutely." He could spend his life watching her. Everything new, as if he were the one ten years older.

"Oh, the chips are warm." She dipped into the salsa, took a bite, coughed. "Oh my! Good!" Eyes watering, she fanned her mouth, then dipped again, glanced at the menu. "You'll have to order for me," she said, "I can't even read the English."

The mariachis strolled over and he had them play Grandma Estella's favorite, surprised they knew it, "*Las Golondrinas.*" He watched her watching them, sipping her margarita, holding it with both hands, licking salt from the rim. He wanted to make love to her now, wondered how far back the seats in the Lamborghini went. The waiter interrupted his thought, and William ordered a sample platter, enchiladas, carne asada fajitas, a small chile *relleno*, *carnitas*, a tamale, extra guacamole.

Julia listened to the words. When the waiter was gone, she leaned forward. "Talk to me in Spanish, William. I love how it sounds."

"Well, that was just food. I don't . . ." He stopped. What the heck. Why disappoint her? She wouldn't know the difference. He lowered his voice, looked into her eyes, spoke the phrase he'd memorized for Nancy Carlton, the only Spanish he knew. "*No te mueves,*" he said. "*Si te mueves o gritas, yo tendré que hacerte daño.*"

He heard a sound, turned to look. A boy with a water pitcher was behind his shoulder, eyes wide, then he hurried toward the kitchen. William shrugged.

"Oh, say it again," Julia said, "it's beautiful, William." She moved her tongue slowly along the rim, smiling, and he felt himself getting hard. "Again, please," she begged, playful. "I love it."

"*No te mueves o gritas . . . si te mueves yo tendré que hacerte. . .*" A hand gripped his shoulder.

"*Joven, ven conmigo. Necesito hablar contigo. Ahorita!*"

That clenched-teeth sound, low, not to disturb other guests. William had no idea what the words meant, but the tone was clear. He turned and faced a belt buckle almost exactly like the one he'd left on Nancy Carlton's floor yesterday morning. He looked up. The guy was in his fifties, black hair flecked silver at the temples, burly, biceps flexing under tight white sleeves. Big Chalino mustache, *bolo* tie. Fuck, William thought. Probably packing too. The boy with the pitcher was standing beside the man, smug. Little *rata*. He knew that word.

"I'm sorry," William said, "I don't speak Spa . . ." He glanced at Julia, her eyes questioning. "I mean, my Spanish isn't that good. What did you say?"

"*Pinche pendejo.* What shit are you trying to pull here?" The guy looked across at Julia. "Excuse me, señora, but I heard. Nobody talks like this to a woman, not in my place. You know this man? Is he threatening you?"

The hand tightened, squeezing the muscle above William's collarbone. It hurt like hell. The guy glanced at the bandage on William's forehead as if he was about to give it a good thump, and William winced, his head throbbing suddenly. He was afraid he'd have to throw a punch, gorilla biceps or not.

Julia saw. "I met him yesterday," she said to the man, smiling. She leaned closer. The way she was holding the margarita made her bodice open slightly, revealing cleavage, Minnesota white. "I'm paying him, actually," she whispered, glancing around and back up at the man. He edged closer as if he hadn't heard right. "I'm paying him to have sex with me," she said. William felt the hand loosen on his shoulder, the guy's mouth had probably fallen open. No question where his eyes were. William smiled, amazed. Somehow he managed not to laugh. She was good. Was this what half a margarita did?

Julia leaned farther, more cleavage, her eyes serious, confiding. She was more beautiful than ever, her hair tousled, face bright with mischief, and William thought, the guy is dust. Dust.

"You see," she said, matter-of-factly, "I haven't had sex in a very long time. I was in prison back East . . . it was self defense, but . . . well, I tried with my cellmate a few times, but it isn't the same, you know, so when I got out I wanted the very best, and . . ." Her voice lifted then. "Are you the owner here?" She licked the rim slowly, took another drink.

Evidently the man could not speak. He might've been nodding, but William couldn't take his eyes off Julia to find out.

"Because I just love this place," she went on, "it's so romantic, the fountain and music, and all this color, this gorgeous wood!" She ran her hand over the table. "You've really done a wonderful job here." She looked up, nodded. "And do you know, I have never had Mexican food. Not in my whole life. And here I am, celebrating. And what I'd really, really love right now," she emptied her glass, "is another of these drinks. What do you call them?"

The guy cleared his throat. "*Una . . . ma . . . margarita*," he stammered. "*Si. . . ahorita*, and your dinner. I will bring it now." He glanced at William, a kind of awe in his eyes. "And we have dancing at ten o'clock," he said. "That is, if you can . . . if you would like to wait."

Forty-six

When the guy was gone they looked at each other, grinning. William shook his head. "Man! You . . . you're something!"

Julia whispered, "What did you say that made him so angry?" But before he could answer the waiter brought a large platter and two plates, and the owner himself was back with margaritas.

"On the house," he said, and motioned the mariachis to their table. "A toast, señora," he added, handing them each a glass. "*Salud, dinero y amor, y tiempo para gastarlos.* Health, señora, money, love, and time to enjoy them." He stole another glance at Julia's bodice.

"*Gracias,*" she said.

William served her portions so she could taste everything. What would he tell her? The truth, he decided. After all, half of her story just now was true, maybe all if you took it metaphorically, maybe even the cellmate part. He was getting hard again. But he couldn't exactly explain with these guys standing here in their tight studded pants singing *corridos.*

"Oh, this is delicious!" Julia said. "What's this one?"

"Enchilada," he said.

He scooped grilled fajita meat, onions and bell peppers into a tortilla, showed her how to fold the end so the contents wouldn't spill out. They ate, sipped margaritas. Maybe if she got tipsy enough she'd forget the question. Not likely. The medley ended, he handed the leader a twenty and they strolled off to another table.

"Well?" Julia said.

So he told her about Nancy Carlton. A thousand dollars, cash, weekly. And how she wanted him to talk Spanish, rough, her break-and-enter fantasy. He had asked a friend, memorized the phrase she wanted, "Don't move. If you move or scream I'll have to hurt you." And then he told how she'd treated him like a houseboy. Walking her damn dog. "I'm not going back," he said finally. "I might start grad school again, get on with my life. I think I'm done with this 'career.'" He waited, watched her face. He wanted to tell her about Wainwright's offer, but not yet. The last thing Julia needed was empty talk. Besides, no one decided to change a whole life in a weekend.

She smiled. "Not before tonight, I hope. I still have some cash, you know."

He laughed. Leaned back and just laughed. This woman.

"So, William," she said then, "you don't know Spanish. But do you dance?" She moved her shoulders with the music. "Because I'd love to try. Just a little. What time is it?"

He checked his watch. "Nine fifteen. And, yes, of course I can dance. I am Mexican. Mexicans are born dancing."

"Mmm." She nodded, licked the rim of her glass, held his eyes. "So what shall we do for the next forty-five minutes?"

Forty-seven

The Lamborghini's seats went back far enough, all right. He checked to be sure, then drove around into the alley. Sealed in shadows, the windows narrow slivers, no one could see in anyway. And this time William kept to his rule. It wasn't easy holding back, but this was just play. The whole night was ahead. Twelve hours, maybe fourteen. Check-out time probably noon. The ceiling was so low they seemed pinned together, could move only inches. It was enough.

"Julia," he whispered against her neck.

"I know," she breathed, "I know."

*   *   *

The dance floor was past the dining room in another open courtyard, larger than the one off the entrance. A platform of polished wood planks bolted securely to the pavers. Only half a dozen other couples, summer, off season. A different band than inside, salsa, Tex-Mex, a little Cuban tossed in.

He taught her the *cumbia* first; you dance apart, easy rhythm, like riding a horse, arms up, holding the reins.

"It's been a while since I rode a horse," she said, laughing. "Thirty years. My grandfather had a farm near Oskaloosa. Raised Morgans."

"Oska what?"

But how she took to the dance. Man. "I think maybe you're part Mexican," William said.

She laughed. "My grandfather on my mother's side used to say we were a little bit Kickapoo Indian. We never knew if he was kidding. It's an actual tribe in Minnesota, you know."

"There's a street called Kickapoo in Yucca Valley. I didn't know it was a real name."

No surprise, how well they could dance together, how their bodies fit. Awkward only the first minutes as he showed her the steps. Margaritas helped, of course, although she changed to ice water after the second number.

"Oh my," she said, following his feet.

"You've done this before, haven't you?" He laughed.

"Never. But oh, oh my gosh!"

When the music changed to a *ranchera* Julia kicked off her sandals, braced on his shoulders, their hands clasped straight to their sides, and they moved in a circle on the wood planks. Faster as the music speeded up. She threw her head back, feet hardly touching the floor, the room a blur, purple bougainvillea, whitewashed walls, stars.

They returned to their table only to gulp water and go again, breathless. Cuban waltzes helped. And finally the *banda*.

"The *banda* is as close as you can get to making love in public," William said.

"You want me to do that?" She watched another couple, kids.

Julia clung to his shoulders with both hands, and once they got the rhythm, he lifted her thigh to his waist, her skirt hiked up, rocking back and forth, dipping her almost to the floor. She could feel him hard against her, her knees trembly.

"Are you sure you don't have a little Mexican in you?" he whispered.

She laughed. "I will later, if I'm lucky."

Then she noticed the restaurant owner and two waiters standing in the doorway, staring. She blushed. "Maybe we should go, William. I'm sweating, and I need to get out of this dress."

Another song started. "That's a *huapango*, anyway," he said, "if we try the *huapango* we'll definitely never make it through the rest of the night." He tossed a look at the men, his hand on Julia's back, steering her out a side exit.

Forty-eight

11:43. The grotto pool was empty. Sunday night, most of the guests gone. Completely still, no breeze rustling the palms, no hum of cicadas, only the waterfall. A silent moon playing in the ripples.

Julia slipped her hand from William's, walked to the steps. She would memorize this, every leaf and petal, the pale blue coating, the darker corridor to the shallow pool, the ledge across, where she had lurked, reptilian. The night they saw the white owl. Last night. Could it be?

William watched. He had felt the change in her as they drove the few miles back. She hadn't spoken, simply leaned against the leather, eyes closed, but not asleep, he knew. He sensed something gathering in her, a heightened intensity. It was like standing near a large transformer, the buzz of current inaudible, yet you feel it.

She moved only her hands now, undid the ribbons at her shoulders, the hooks and eyes, let her dress fall to her feet, didn't step out of it. She stood completely still, naked, her face tilted slightly, hands open at her sides, as if to draw in the world, a Hindu statue with eyes in her palms and forehead. Skin glistening white.

William slipped off his clothes, waited.

Here the Hidden Springs magic might work again, Julia thought, time would slow, rewind, maybe. Close her eyes, and when she opened them it would be yesterday, and she'd be sitting at the table in front of her "cabin," and he'd be walking toward her down the path, stepping onto the little stone bridge. Begin all over. A calm started in her center and moved up. She could have that anytime now. The moments were all hers, and more still to make.

She walked down the steps, lowered herself in, submerged, came up, water streaming, smoothing her hair back. She drew a deep breath, swam the length underwater, thirty feet or so, slowly, fingers splayed. Like moving through liquid silk. No one really swam in the grotto, just soaked, but with it all to herself . . . she went again, edged along the smooth bottom, eyes open to watch how the moon shimmered the water. She surfaced and dipped like an otter, easy, slow, then back, her skin gauging warm and cooler pockets. And again, turning beneath the waterfall, hotter there, very hot.

There was no way to capture this, William thought, standing on the edge, patient. The light mottling the surface, a dozen shades, blue to white, her body gliding back and forth, distorted as if she herself had turned to liquid, a water sprite all but disappearing in the shadows. He would not intrude. It would be like disturbing someone at prayer.

Finally she surfaced, close where she could touch bottom. She gasped for breath, wiped her eyes, smoothed her hair. Then she held up her hands to him, beckoning, and he walked down the steps and took her in his arms.

Forty-nine

They found towels on a bench, wrapped in them, and walked the path to the stone "cabin." But as Julia reached to unlock the door, William touched her arm. "Not yet," he said, "the night's too beautiful to go inside. Let's walk by the lake. Want to?"

She looked past him to the stars, smiled. "Yes, of course." When else would she get to walk under such a sky? The air perfect, not the slightest chill even with her hair wet from the pool.

William set their clothes and shoes on the table, took her

hand, and they went barefoot down the path, crossing the stream back and forth, wearing only the thick white towels.

She sensed more in his thoughts, but didn't ask. They had all night. And the last time she followed his whim they ended up in Al Capone's tunnel! The thought made a billowing in her chest as if she might rise off the ground and twirl away. She leaned close and hugged his arm with both hands. Ballast.

William was remembering their talk at the oasis and something he once read, something he wanted to give her if he could. Didn't compare with what she had given him, set his mind buzzing, ideas connecting. *Linear. Rational. Progress.* Rethinking Hannah Arendt! Love transcends rationality. *The greatest of these is love.* Hadn't the line between philosophy and religion always blurred? Boethius. Thomas Aquinas. And now science. Quantum physics. He wanted to do research again, find a library, reread certain books. He wanted to browse the stacks, cross-reference. He wanted to Google.

He grinned. But first this. And it would work best outside. Beyond the lower pond was a secluded spot with soft grass.

The moon was high over the lake now, light filtering through the tall tamarisks, reflecting off the ripples. Music drifted from a distant bungalow, and laughter. The whine of a golf cart off toward the front gate, then quiet.

"Over there," William said as they passed the waterfall

that fed the smaller pond. "That's where the water sinks back into the earth."

A slight breeze prickled her skin. Where he pointed she could see only darkness.

They left the lighted path and followed the stream across the grass until it disappeared into a clump of shrubs and low trees, unkempt. The air breathed the musk of plant life gone wild, warm mineral water soaking the ground, the grass thick and cushiony beneath their feet. They stood in a swath of moonlight not far from the edge of the Hidden Springs compound. Beyond was open desert, and Julia could just make out the contour of sand dunes dotted with creosote and sage, fading to black.

William led her into the shadows where the grass made a small knoll, hardly a foot high, almost like a grave. Yes, here, this would do nicely.

"Julia."

He drew her close, kissed her softly, just once, but the heat was instant, lightning bursts under her ribs, her body ignited as if it were made of straw. Yes, she thought, oh, take me, hard, now! Yes! But before she could speak, he pulled back, his hand on her cheek.

"Julia, there's something I want to give you, something I've never done for anyone. It's different." He smiled. "A kind of journey. Will you go with me?"

"Anywhere." She stared into the darkness. "Are we going into the desert? Don't we need shoes?"

He laughed. "No, here. A journey of the mind." He took the towel from his waist, spread it over the grassy mound, then stood back.

She gasped. Different, yes. They had known each others' bodies in various ways, and yet now to see him standing naked in the dim light. So beautiful. Magnificent, a template of what a man's body should be. Shoulders to waist and down. Never in her life had she thought of a penis as lovely, but it was, there peaceful against his thigh.

He waited. And when she met his eyes again, he smiled. "So will you join me?" He nodded for her to drop her towel. "Just lie there on the grass. I'll be your guide."

Sweet Jesus! His voice, his eyes. Her knees gone liquid. She might melt into the earth.

He came to her, undid her towel, lay it over his on the knoll. Then he took her hands, helped her down. "There, now lie back a little more. So your body forms to the curve of the ground."

She scooted farther until her shoulders were at the top of the knoll, her head arched back on the gentle slope. She closed her eyes. How good it felt to stretch naked here in the open, the ground warm against her back. Nipples tingling in the air. Temple priestess on the altar.

William knelt beside her, whispered, "Open your eyes."

Stars, nothing but stars! An immense canopy. Like that Egyptian painting, the great mother goddess arched over the earth, her body studded with stars.

William took a deep breath, exhaled. "Just relax, breathe. Let me take you there. I'm not going to touch you. Only words. You'll see. And then you'll always have this. You can go there whenever you want."

He was quiet for some time. She waited, drifting with the night sky. No hurry. She was tired, yet every cell was alive with anticipation, *go there whenever you want*, the air caressing her bare skin. She thought of the earth beneath her, and deeper, the subterranean lake, hot, drawing up through the strata. Gaia holding her, lifting her hips, rocking.

And then William's words. By now she should expect the unexpected. Linear. What did linear have to do with the journey? Didn't produce the slightest tingle. Except the sound of his voice. Passion. Yes, she could see him in a university lecture hall, tweed jacket, students rapt. He was taking up their conversation from this afternoon at the oasis. She smiled, remembering.

"Linear. That's it," he was saying, "the faulty premise, the reason the world is such a mess. The idea that human systems go forward in a straight line, always improving, each more 'civilized' than the last. And, of course, the most 'civilized' has the most rights," he gave a low laugh, "bigger piece of the pie. It's a male premise, power and thrust, conquest, war, hierarchies. And it's all wrong." He paused.

She wanted to look at him, but to move would break the spell. Stars, concentrate on the stars. She wanted to spread her legs, let the stars enter her. *Relax. Let me take you there.*

When he spoke again there was a sadness in his voice. "The world has been broken for a long, long time," he said, "and we're conditioned to think it's just the way it is, the way it must be, because we've forgotten. There will always be war, always poverty, injustice, abuse. And I think every woman senses how wrong that is, the fundamental lie. Maybe not consciously, but it's there, and it causes a deep loneliness. For men too. I mean, how can you have true intimacy with an inferior? Or worse, a possession?" His voice was a whisper. "And we wonder why it's so hard to make love last."

She wanted to hold him. Never mind the journey. She braced her hands on the ground to sit up. Not easy the way she was arched back. Then she felt his hand on her abdomen.

"No, stay there," he said. "We're just starting. I want to show you a power you have in your body, here, your center." He moved his hand slightly and she felt the sweet pressure. "You don't even need touch," he said. But he didn't take his hand away.

"Ah. The moon, see? See what the moon is doing?"

She looked. It had topped the trees, and the swath of light had moved over them.

"My God, you are so beautiful," he said, and she could hear the smile in his voice, his hand moving slowly on her abdomen. She felt the spread of his fingers radiating through her, calm, yet fire. Five points. She could feel a gentle pull inside, there beneath his hand. A tugging reaching down, down, the way it felt when a baby nursed, a delicious throbbing.

"This right here is the answer," he said, "all along." His hand made a gentle circle. "The womb is the pattern. It could heal the world if we understood that." His voice excited now, thoughts gelling to words.

She felt him move closer, his hand circling slow, sending pulses deep inside, as if he had entered her not between her legs, but from her womb, her center. She arched more, the ground hard beneath her body, the pressure of his fingers. Her eyes wide. The stars, yes, the moon. Sensations rippling soft, expanding. Shudders. How could this be happening? She gasped.

"Think of it, Julia. Nothing in nature is linear. It is all based on the circle. Cycles, birth, death, rebirth, the orbit of the planets, ocean currents, weather, water rising into rain, even our cells, electrons spinning." His voice rose, and she with it. "There is no straight line in nature," he said. "None. It's all connected and connected, circles within circles. All sacred, all part of the universe, part of God. And not a single element or being is better than another. As if a worm were less than a tree or a lion. How stupid is that? Only man in his pride thinks himself a king."

A moan escaped her lips, and she gasped, his thoughts spinning her, his voice. Vibrations through the tips of his fingers, deep, from inside, couldn't get any deeper. Pulses turning to throbs, spasms. Her eyes drinking the stars. Oh my God. Oh my God!

He leaned forward. "Julia, what is it? You're not . . . But I didn't even . . ."

She smiled, breathed, wanted to cry out, yet controlling it made it last. What had he said? Something about a king.

William reached to hold her, and she found her voice. "No. Don't stop. Your hand. Oh, Jesus!" How could it last so long? She swallowed, breathed, let it take her. A wave, a glorious long wave, swelling, carrying her. Up, up, into the canopy. Until it washed over her completely, set her on the sand. She smiled, closed her eyes.

All connected. No one part better than another. Last shudders, the ebb rocking her gently, a tiny shell on the shore of an inland sea.

She sighed. "Hold me, William. Now you can hold me."

He lifted her, held her against his chest.

She grinned, laughing, wiping the tears. "I can't believe. How could you do that?"

William smiled. Amazing, just when he thought he understood the mystery of the female body and mind. He had planned a whole other list of images to take her there. He kissed her eyes, her cheeks. "Some journey." He laughed. "You went on ahead, left me in the dust, and that's good. That's good. But it wasn't me."

"Oh, yes. Yes, it was. It will always be you."

Fifty

A hush settled over them as they walked back. It was as if they had visited each other in a dream, shared some phenomenon that words might dissolve.

Their clothes were on the patio table. As Julia opened the "cabin" door it felt like reentering the earth's atmosphere. Everything changed, nothing changed.

The clock on the mantle said 12:26. It's still working, she thought, the Hidden Springs time warp. Less than twelve hours now.

A tray with a decanter and cups was on the night stand.

They had called earlier from the restaurant. Coffee. Coffee was real.

She turned to William. He was staring at the case in the chair where he had left it. Might've been a rattlesnake coiled.

The ol' "goodie case," William thought. Relic from his past. That's how it seemed now.

"You forgot that yesterday," she said.

"Yes, well, it's . . ."

"I know." She smiled. "I looked. It wasn't locked. You left out a lot of stories, didn't you?"

"Mmm . . . maybe another time. And did anything there interest you?" Shit, he didn't want to say that. The thing sitting there mocking him, proof of his stupidity. Offering women diversion, that's all, when they should have been fixing their lives. Not so easy, fixing a life.

"One item," Julia said, teasing, "a little interesting. Maybe later." *Another time. Later.* As if they had days and weeks instead of hours.

"Would you like some coffee?" he said, walking across. "It's still hot."

"Oh, yes. We'll have coffee in bed, but we won't sleep."

They found more pillows in the armoire and sat side by side sipping their coffee. Quiet. The clock ticking, cold, indifferent, even Hidden Springs time couldn't be stopped.

"William," she said then, "what did you mean before when you said the world is broken? Hasn't it always been this way?"

He smiled. He hadn't thought his talk even registered. Hardly blame her, considering. And it had been as much for himself, the foundation for his "gift."

"Ah, the human nature argument." He laughed. "Like we can't do any better. But there's evidence," he said, "quite a lot, actually, of people who had a whole different mind-set. They've found ruins of ancient civilizations. Goddess cultures. Whole cities in Europe and Turkey, Romania, all the way to India. Hundreds, I think. They had mastered farming and architecture, commerce. They had sea-going ships. And art, amazing art. Eight thousand years ago. I don't remember the names of the digs. Crete survived the longest, the Minoans."

He paused, thinking. "What were the titles? *The Chalice and the Blade*. That was the main one. But the thing is, they never found any weapons of war or any kind of fortifications. No murals glorifying battle. No statues or pottery or mosaics with warriors taking prisoners. All their art was based on nature. That seemed the central belief, a oneness with nature and, from what they can tell, any surplus went to make life better, not for . . ."

"But wasn't that before metal?" she interrupted. "Maybe they just didn't have the technology for war. It just seems too good to be true, William." Minutes ticking away and they're talking theories and studies, ideas. And it felt good. When had she and Ralph had such a discussion? Never.

"I know," he said, "but plenty of tribes warred against each other without metal. You don't need metal to make a lance or arrows or clubs." He sipped his coffee. "What you need is motivation, or maybe *license* is a better word, whatever makes man think he can have the power to cause death and destruction. We're so used to seeing the world as it is now. It takes a huge shift in thinking. The first archeologists didn't even make the connection." His voice changed. "Let's see, they were just too uncivilized for war. Too primitive. Yeah, that's it."

He laughed, turned to her. "How fucked up we are. All the evidence points to a belief system that simply didn't include plundering and killing. And the archeologists ignore the main difference. The Mother Goddess." He held out his hand, as if weighing the facts. "I mean, several thousand years of no war, a people who believe the creative force is female, nurturing, and women are equal partners, now wouldn't you think that might be the key?"

She smiled. "Well, I would, yes." That passion again.

How she loved listening to him. She would find the books. Oh, she was good at finding books.

"And something else," he went on, "in all those sites they never found any sign of a ruling class. They were matriarchies, mainly in terms of lineage, not power. There were no palaces, no elaborate tombs full of gold and chariots and jeweled scepters. No mummies buried with the wives and slaves who had to die with them. As far as we can tell, Julia, these people had no kings."

"*Hamlet*!" she said suddenly, sitting forward, jarring the bed.

"What?" He managed not to spill his coffee.

"Kings. I just remembered. What you said before, how in nature no part is better than another. The lion and the worm thing. There's a line from *Hamlet*. After he kills Polonius. Something about a worm eating of a king . . . a king passing through the guts of a beggar." She smiled, pleased with herself. "Shakespeare, leave it to Shakespeare."

He looked at her and laughed, shaking his head.

"Julia." He set their cups on the night stand. "Come here, you. Enough of all that. Kiss me. Just kiss me." He would send her the books. Amazon, no way to trace. He pulled her onto his chest and kissed her, playing. Rolling like puppies, laughing, kissing, nuzzling. Real kisses.

He wanted to erase every technique, every calculated move, every empty rule. Kissing was a luxury, something you rarely did with a client. Never real kissing.

The difference was infinite.

He loved her. Yes. That they could not say the words, did not matter.

Fifty-one

To stay awake they traded childhood stories. How he had lived with his Grandma Estella until he was four, while his mother got her life together, came back finally with his stepfather, George, and his new baby sister. His mother left again when he was thirteen, and by then he'd forgotten his Spanish. He had a tiny memory of riding in the locomotive with his great grandpa before he died, or maybe it was Grandma Estella's telling it he remembered, hardly more than two years old at the time.

Julia told how her father would take her with him ice fishing, bundled so tight she toppled over once in the little shed and couldn't get up, had to wait 'til he pulled in the fish, thirty-pound walleyed pike, flopping all around, bigger than she was.

And later, after more coffee, she told how she'd nursed her babies fourteen months each, weaned all three right to the cup as her mother-in-law instructed. " 'No bottles for our babies,' she'd say." Julia laughed. "Like a bumper sticker." *Our*, Julia thought. As if she were there in the stirrups with me. "I was so determined. I was a clockwork mom and wife." She looked down. "I'd do it much differently now."

"How old are your kids?" William asked.

"Twenty-four, twenty-two and nineteen. Janet's in college, Matthew went off with a bluegrass band to West Virginia." She smiled. "He's happy. Music is all he seems to need. And our oldest, Elizabeth, is married to an attorney in Cleveland. She's expecting in November."

Julia set her cup on the night stand, nestled against his chest.

There was something else William wanted to ask, but he took his time, considering just how to put the words.

"Tell me, Julia," he said, after several minutes, "why did you come here? I mean, why not just meet someone in a bar or anywhere. A woman like you. You certainly wouldn't have to look far, if it was just sex."

She thought a moment. "Control, maybe. I haven't

had much control in my life. But not just that. I wanted it to be clean."

"Clean?" He tried to see her eyes, but she was leaning against his chest, looking up at the skylight.

"Yes, clean. Honest," she said, smiling. "You know, like what you said before about integrity. Because the other is a lie, you know. The whole romance thing. What men mainly want is sex and then, well, ownership. Like what you said. It goes back a long time. Romance is just how they get there."

William listened. It wasn't bitterness in her voice, more like acceptance.

She sat up, turned to him. "Like Lucille, my sister. She's been married three times, a line of lovers in between, and she says it's always good at first. She's an investment broker. It got so she measured the success of a relationship by how many assets she had to sign over to get out of it." Julia laughed. "She's back in Oskaloosa, restoring our grandfather's old place. She keeps cats . . . and the occasional farmhand."

Julia hugged a pillow to her chest. "My life was completely different," she said, "but I wouldn't call it honest. Whatever they say, being married doesn't make it honest. More like playing parts, for us anyway, only we didn't even have the same script." She sighed. "The only true honesty is being who you really are, and how can you know that when you're . . ." She looked up at him. She would not say, "when you're young." She had known years ago, but there were children to raise. "Anyway, it changes, that's all. It always changes."

He didn't speak.

She closed her eyes tightly. "Goodness," she said, "going on like that. I don't know what got into me."

"A little Mexican," he said, laughing. "And I hope you're not sorry."

She sat up again. "My God, William, I'm only sorry that . . ." She stopped, her eyes filling. Stupid tears!

"What?"

"That there isn't more time." She bit her lip. "There should be more time."

"Mmm."

He drew her to him, her head beneath his chin, ran his hand over her hair. "You know what I think?" he said. "I think people don't really decide much about . . . . these things." He almost said "love." That word again. "I think," he went on, "we simply do what we must. What we can't not do."

He held her. Julia. He didn't even know her real name.

In minutes he felt her relax against his chest. Her breathing changed, and he leaned back, closed his eyes.

Fifty-two

The phone was ringing. Julia groped for the receiver. Five fifteen, the recording said, the wake-up call she had ordered, just in case.

She lay back, fully awake now, her heart suddenly racing, stomach tight. The skylight was beginning to color, lily pads and big pinkish white flowers. "The lark," she thought, "herald of the morn." Shakespeare again, his doomed lovers.

Damn! Three hours wasted. She turned, her eyes filling with tears.

William was awake, watching her.

He pulled her to him, tilted her chin, kissed her eyes. Too

early to try Wainwright, William thought. Wait until eight o'clock. Seven thirty at the earliest. It wasn't the career he wanted, but what the hell. It'd be temporary, a transition, that's all.

"Not yet," he whispered, "*shh*, not yet."

She breathed in, nodded, wiped her eyes. He was right. Yes.

He smiled. "So, tell me, Julia, which item did you find interesting?" He was buying time. If he could just get something solid to offer, then he'd lay it all out, let her decide. See which won, her cynical theories or what he saw in her eyes. He'd bet on her eyes.

"Item?" she said.

He gestured to the chair. "In the case, you know."

"Now?"

"Why not? If you want. Checkout isn't until noon. You weren't thinking of leaving early, were you?"

"No!"

Love, William thought. Sure, the odds are against it. Odds are against winning the lottery too, but people still keep buying tickets.

Fifty-three

When the phone rang again, Julia groaned. "Oh, let it ring, just another wake-up call, probably." She couldn't see the clock. Didn't care.

William was in front of her, between her legs, which were bent almost to her chest. He was holding her feet, one in each hand, rubbing them with his thumbs.

Not bad, William thought. It was a position he'd just invented. He was inside her, up on his knees, thrusting steadily, her hips supported by mountains of pillows. Her wrists were tied to the bedposts with silk scarves, the one "item of interest" she'd chosen from his goodie case, and she'd been laughing, how this had to be the ultimate luxury, a foot rub while screwing, helpless to do anything but enjoy.

"Just a little multitasking, ma'am," he said now, his Sean Connery voice, rubbing the balls of her feet, keeping his slow rhythm. He amazed even himself sometimes.

"Oh my." She laughed, curled her toes. "Who would imagine?"

That damned phone was distracting, though. Finally the ringing stopped.

A minute passed, and it started again.

Julia glanced up at her right hand, a pink silk bow at the wrist, then at William. "Could you stop that phone?" she said, laughing. "I'm a little tied up."

He placed her right foot against his chest to free his hand. Leaning, he could just reach the receiver. He picked it up, set it quickly back in place, resumed his "multitasking," Julia giggling.

The look in her eyes, William thought, like Lois Lane when Superman sweeps her away on her first flight. Pity to come up with such a move just when he was abandoning the profession. Could've made a fortune on this alone. Could've been his trademark. No, he thought, this is Julia's. Even if she refused his offer, he'd keep it for her. She'd come back, once a year, maybe. . . .

The phone rang again.

They looked at each other. William stopped.

"I guess we should see," she said. It must be Lucille. No one else knew where she was. It was almost seven thirty.

William repeated the foot-on-the-chest maneuver to free his hand. He leaned and lifted the receiver, held it to Julia's ear.

At first she just listened, expecting the wake-up recording, the thing probably set to redial until it got a real voice. But the line was silent, except . . . . breathing. Was that breathing? Her smile faded. Was it possible to recognize breathing. Don't be silly.

She listened a moment more, closed her eyes, a sudden tightening in her chest. How could it be? It could not.

Faintly she said, "Hello?"

"I know where you are, and I know what you're doing, bitch."

Fifty-four

A whimper started in Julia's throat, but she kept it back. No. Give him nothing.

Eyes wide, wrists bound, she listened as William held the phone. Fine torture, a corner of her mind thought, tie her up, have her husband spew venom in her ear.

Such words! Fucking bitch. God damned lying cunt. If she was holding the receiver herself, she'd have flung it far. Cyanide pellet tossed into the room, live grenade. Her heart hammering so loud he might hear.

What did she expect? Ralph to suggest they talk out their problems, maybe try one of those sensitivity seminars for couples? She'd heard him go on like this down at the yard with the men, rarely to her or the kids. But then she'd been smart over the years, a very clever mouse, scurry all the way to the pantry without disturbing a whisker.

Yelling. Owner of a large, successful business and oh, yes, a hunting lodge on Muskeg Bay, and he still swore like a trucker. She met William's eyes, almost smiled. Bitch. Cunt. What a tiny price to pay . . .

My God, she must be in shock. This was serious.

"Desert fucking Hot Springs," Ralph yelled. "Did you think I wouldn't figure it out? Not a chance. Not a fucking chance. Doesn't take Einstein to retrieve deleted files, make a few calls. Or did you think I was too stupid?"

He paused, waiting.

What calls? Lucille, the dealership? It was too early for the dealership. And Lucille would never . . . He was bluffing. All he knew was that she was here. She should say something, anything. But she couldn't seem to form a single syllable. What? I didn't mean to hurt you, Ralph. I just needed some time away. Right. Considering the position she was in, tied to the damned bedposts, William holding her left foot, the other against his chest. Julia pulled her feet down, scooted her lower body back toward the headboard. All she could do. Straining the ties at her wrists.

William followed, holding the phone to her ear, his eyes

stunned, mouthing, "What? What?" With his free hand he untied the scarves. An accident? he thought, one of her children hurt or killed? But the voice on the phone was yelling.

She could not answer. She deserved this, of course. No defense. Bitch and cunt. Next it'd be slut, whore. Men got all the really good names. Was that it? She had needed to do something so bad that the decision would be made for her?

Only when Ralph mentioned the children did it start to sink in. She felt sick.

William saw her eyes change, so stricken, her face drained. He pulled the phone away, listened. Ah, yes, the husband. He wanted to answer, say something appropriate, but, no. He set the receiver on the nightstand as it ranted on. Thank God, he thought. At least no one had died. He moved to Julia, tried to take her in his arms, but she pushed him away, her eyes steely now.

"I have to make a call," she whispered. She scrambled to the phone, hung it up, but when she lifted the receiver again, Ralph was still on the line.

"Answer me, damn it. I know you're there. You better fucking answer me! I'm coming out there. I'll find you! I will, and believe me . . ."

She slammed the phone back down, stared, tried to think. He was bluffing.

William was off the bed and back with his cell phone.

She dialed, hands shaking. Breathing in, she waited for her sister to pick up. Sunday morning. She'd be home.

"Lucille, did Ralph call you? Did you tell him anything?"

"Of course not. You know I'd never do that."

"Well, he found something on my computer, I guess. He called here. Said he's coming, but I doubt that. Anyway, I'm all right. I'll be checking out soon, and then . . . I'm not sure. Things have changed . . ." She was careful not to look at William. "And Lucille, could you call the kids? Tell them . . . Oh, I don't know, not to listen to . . ."

Lucille laughed that laugh of hers. "Heavens," she said, "who listens to Ralph? And he doesn't know anything. You took a trip, that's all. After twenty-five years, you can take a trip. Sure, I'll talk to the kids. They know how he is."

Lucille, the businesswoman. Always cool. "Thanks," Julia said. "Tell them I'll call soon when I . . . figure things out."

Julia fell back against the pillows.

William watched her face.

Lucille was right, Julia thought. What could Ralph really know? That she had lied about going to Oskaloosa. That she was in California at an expensive resort. Adults only. The room was registered under Lucille's name. Not so hard to figure out. And perhaps . . . perhaps he knew that she had saved the photograph of a handsome young man in her recipe folder. Oyster soufflé.

A smile started again. She put her hand to her mouth. What was wrong with her?

William sat beside her, helpless. He was losing her, he knew, could feel her slipping away. Tied to the damned bedposts, fucking, when her husband called. Shit. How she must feel. It was over, he didn't have a chance. Sitting here naked, the two of them.

But what was she doing now?

On the nightstand, Julia found the Hidden Springs number, dialed the office on William's cell. What was it Grandpa Lawrence used to say? Might as well be hung for a sheep as a lamb. Ralph said he was coming here. What if he was already on a plane? He could be driving out from L.A. right now. He could be at the gate. She shuddered.

"A man has been calling my room," she told the operator. "I don't know him. I think he's still on the line. Please don't put him through again. Don't put any calls through. And could you tell them at the gate? I'll be checking out soon."

She clicked off, stayed quiet for a moment. She thought of how it would be, walking back into the house, telling her lies, and when he finally calmed down, then what?

She turned to William, shrugged. "I can't go back," she said. "I don't have the slightest idea what I'll do. I just know I can't go back. Not ever."

She shook her head, and then she could no longer control

it, she smiled. Jesus! A twenty-five-year marriage, her house, furniture, clothes, everything, gone. Oh, she would see the kids. They were grown, he couldn't keep her from them. And Lucille was right. The children knew how it was. Children always know.

Still, she should not be smiling. She must be in shock, one of those involuntary reactions, like laughing at a funeral. Crazy. Round-the-bend crazy. Next she'd be up dancing.

Fifty-five

They sat looking at each other.

She had decided. Not exactly the decision William had hoped for, more a running from than a running to. He had wanted to offer her something calm and clear and possible. Still, it was up to him now. Who knew what the guy would do if he found her? He had to get her away from here, someplace safe. His apartment? No. Any detective could track them there. The Hidden Springs gatehouse had his license plate number.

He needed to take her and leave. They'd stop at his bank. He could get five or six thousand fast. The rest would take longer. He glanced at the clock, an idea forming, almost eight o'clock. "We should hurry." He did not say what he was thinking. They didn't know where her husband had called from.

"I have a few thousand dollars," she said. "I'm sure he'll cut off my cards soon. Maybe if I go to an ATM now, I can get cash before . . ." Her eyes wavered. She should not bring William into this. Husbands went crazy sometimes. Newspapers were full of stories. If he tracked them down. If something happened to William because of her . . .

"I could go stay at my sister's in Oskaloosa," she said. A moment ago she had been so sure. But now. Maybe she should just go back. She had thought this time with William would be enough, live it over and over in her mind. Better if she had never walked onto that plane.

No, never that! Better to just get into the Lamborghini now, drive as fast as it would go. Find a bridge. Do a Thelma and Louise. Okay, just a Thelma.

William touched her cheek. "Julia, I'm not letting you go. Not if I can help it. I want to be with you. I . . ." He stopped. He knew her theories. *Beginnings are always good. Then it changes.* Be careful. "And there is a way," he said, "if you're up for it."

"What? Oh, anything. Anything! Tell me!" How she sounded. Like Juliet reaching for the potion. But they were not teenagers. This was not one of her books or a damned movie. If she was doomed, she would not take William with her.

"Well," William said slowly, "there's always Mexico." He took a breath, smiled. "Do you know how long we could live in Mexico on a Lamborghini Murcielago?"

Fifty-six

Julia stared at him. *We.* Do you know how long *we* could live in Mexico . . . What was he saying?

He saw the shock in her eyes, started again. "Or maybe that's not such a good idea, stealing a car . . ."

"It wouldn't be stealing," she said quietly. My God, he'd said *we.* Julia smiled.

"What do you mean?"

"I leased it to the business account. It's in both our names." She'd put fifty-eight thousand down, the exact amount of her inheritance, but it was only on paper. "I planned to take the car back after the weekend, but all I have to do is make a call and change it to a purchase. And he, well," the smile spread to her eyes, "he owes me." A Lamborghini was worth about the same as one of his fancy new belly dumps, and he had a whole fleet. They. They had a whole fleet. Any court would award her at least part of the business. He had used her money to start it. Oh, this might turn out quite nicely. Later she'd go back, get an attorney, a fair settlement. Maybe a certain hunting lodge on Muskeg Bay. She'd turn it into a wildlife refuge.

"Well then," William said, standing, taking her hands, pulling her to her feet. "We still should hurry. You can call from the road." He glanced at her body, smiled. "Clothes might be good. And I have to go to my bank. Pull out my savings. Sign papers to have the rest transferred. I know this place in Rosarito Beach, Baja. You'll love it. It's right on a cliff overlooking two of the most beautiful coves. And, Julia, I didn't tell you . . ." he tried to keep the hesitation out of his voice, "but Charles Wainwright said he might have a job for me. There's a movie studio just past Rosarito. I'll call him on the way, see if he really meant it. Come on."

He grabbed his jeans from the chair by the bed. "I'll explain more on the way." He had one leg in his pants when he noticed she hadn't moved.

She sat back down on the bed.

"No," she said softly, "no. I can't."

Fifty-seven

The look on his face, as if she'd slapped him. He finished pulling on his pants, sat in the chair, his jaw set.

How she wanted to hold him, take the words back. But she could not let him do this. His savings. Trade his future for time with her. Hadn't she done the same thing? A job in a movie studio. That wasn't the life he wanted. But she couldn't say it that way. He'd talk her out of it, and it would be so easy to talk her out of it.

"William . . ." Her voice wavered, and she had to stop, breathe, begin again. "William, this time we've had . . . not even two days. We hardly know each other. And I've been married for twenty-five years. I have a home and children. I . . . I have to go back." She reached, pulled the sheet around her, held it in fists.

It was a lie. She would not go back. She didn't know what she would do, but she would never, ever go back. Only to tie things up, see the children, explain. But not the lie she had just told. There was more she could say. That she was just getting free, she needed to live, see things, learn what it was she really wanted, and, oh, yes, her theories. Beginnings were always good. But then they fade, they always, always fade. Some trick God or the universe plays on us, and she would have no more of it. No more watching it get ugly.

Better to keep their time as it was. Magic. But if she started to think of their hours together . . . the gift he had given her by the lake. She felt the tears and stopped them. There was only one irrefutable argument, and she had said it.

She took another breath, whispered again. "I have to go back, William. I'm sorry."

He sat a long moment, watching her. "You're sure? You've thought this through?"

She looked down. "Yes."

He nodded, stood, pulled on his shirt, his shoes. He went to the other chair, snapped his "goodie case" shut. Debris, that's all it was. Clean up the debris.

He came back, bent, kissed her forehead. To hold her again . . .

"Will you be all right?"

"Yes."

"You'd better go soon, in case . . ."

"Yes, I know." She looked up at him. Tears, impossible to stop. "William . . ."

"*Shh*," he said, "it's okay. It's okay." He touched her cheek.

She closed her eyes, heard only his footsteps. He stopped, seemed to hesitate, but she did not move, and then the door latched shut.

Fifty-eight

She sat starting at the floor, her hands to her mouth. What had she done? What had she done? Her chest heaved, but she would not let the sobs start.

Then the phone rang. She jumped. She had said no calls. William! It might be William on his cell phone. Trembling, she lifted the receiver.

"Yes?"

"I'm sorry to disturb you, Ms. Reeves, but there's a man at the gate. He says he's your husband. He's, well, he's very upset. Says he came all the way from Minnesota. We have security here, and he's calmed down some. We can call the police, if you want." He paused. "We'd rather not have a scene."

She tried to think. My God, Ralph was here! The fear started in her stomach, adrenaline shooting through her chest. He *had* been calling from the road.

Time. She needed time. And then she realized, William was gone. He was safe. He could be driving out the gate right now. Relief flooded over her. She tried not to picture what they had just avoided, but there it was, a sudden clarity she had not seen until this moment. Beyond her betrayal, compounding it: the mere sight of William. His beautiful brown skin. It would have triggered something in Ralph so irrational. Evil. She closed her eyes, saw a vision of blood. But they had slipped past it. By minutes. Some gift of fate.

"Ms. Reeves . . ."

She could not speak. Gripping the sheet, shaking now. Breathe. Think.

"Ms. Reeves. We have an awkward situation here. Is this man your husband?"

She could hear muffled talk, but not yelling. That's how Ralph was, a first flash of rage, then mostly bluster, especially with other people around. Men who didn't work for him. But she had to hurry. She had to catch William. Think.

"We're separated," she said, "and . . . Listen, I need your help. I know it's a lot to ask, but I'm afraid he might be dangerous."

"I can see that. So, the police, then?"

Police. She imagined Ralph in the back of a squad car. He would track her to the ends of the earth. Besides, if he told the police his story, they'd probably look the other way. Direct him to the nearest gun shop.

"No. Tell him . . . Could you tell him I'm in a spa treatment? Could you have him go there and wait?"

Spa treatments were sacred at Hidden Springs. Only death and disaster could make them interrupt a spa treatment. And she had avoided death and disaster . . . so far. Although the way her heart was hammering, it might burst any moment, and that would be that.

No. She wanted to live. Never had she so wanted to live. She must hurry. "If you will do that, I'll pay anyth . . ."

"Ms. Reeves," the voice sounded offended, "you are our guest. At Hidden Springs, the guest always comes first, especially in matters of safety. Security will take him to the spa. I'll have a guard stay with him."

"Thank you." God, thank you! If she could just be out the gate and past the first turn. Julia stood, dropped the sheet, grabbed her sundress from the chair as she spoke, "And one more thing. Would you have Heather meet me in the parking lot?"

"Heather?"

"Yes. Tell her it's very important. I'll be there in just a minute."

Fifty-nine

Julia fastened her dress, grabbed sandals and purse, nothing more. She ran. Monday morning, the grounds deserted. As she passed the entrance to the spa, she saw the golf cart. Security. A guard was ushering Ralph through the open door. Ralph, in his flannel shirt, sleeves rolled up. He did not notice her running past, barefoot on the path.

She felt light, unbearably, exquisitely light, floating. She could pass him, stand directly in front of him, he would not know her. Never had. So trite, to live the wrong life. Everyone thinks that sometimes. But the trick was to let go, walk into another and another. No, not walk, leap. Like the physicist plodding along for years, and in a flash, the solution. Every clumsy step part of it. Clarity. No greater gift. Like the moon rising over the trees. *The world has been broken for a long, long time. Well, not hers. Not anymore.*

At the parking lot she stopped, pulled on her sandals, then hurried across the gravel. Heather was waiting by the Lamborghini. Tank top and shorts, young and tan, and those legs. Perfect.

Julia explained quickly. She opened her purse, held out five one-hundred-dollar bills. Heather's eyes widened. Lovely eyes.

"It won't be easy," Julia said, "but I'd like you to talk him into a massage while he waits. Tell him it's paid for. You might have to calm him down a bit first, get past the good old boy thing. You know, finesse him. Can you do that?"

An hour, they'd be halfway to Mexico.

Heather smiled. "Sure, no problem. I've handled my share of reluctant husbands." She tossed her honey blond hair. "Flirt, a little, cover 'em with a sheet, start oiling, they're all the same, putty."

"Great."

With the guard right there watching, he might actually agree to it. He'd seem an idiot not to. Ralph could be an asshole, Julia thought, but he wasn't dead. Just what he needed, Heather's strong, young hands, working his shoulders and back.

She smiled, closed the bills into Heather's palm. "And if he does go for it, as a special favor, could you do something extra? Oh, nothing too bad. Just something to make him feel a little bit guilty."

Heather's blue eyes twinkled. "You got it. I'll get Megan to help. It'll be fun." She laughed. "We'll massage spots he didn't know he had. He'll be a new man."

Sixty

The Lamborghini spun gravel, and Julia let off the throttle, passed the gatehouse. At the street, she turned left and punched it. My God! Thrown back against the leather, she gripped the wheel.

It had been only minutes since William left, five, six. Drive! She glanced in the rearview mirror, the road behind empty.

She did not slow, even at the edges of Desert Hot Springs. Up ahead, an intersection, the light was green. The tires squealed as she made the turn onto Palm Drive, the long, open stretch to the freeway. A few cars on the road.

She wove around one after another, as if they were standing still, the drivers' eyes wide, passengers turning to glance behind her. Exotic sports car pushing a hundred, must be a chase. Drug bust. Or someone rushing to make a flight out of Palm Springs.

She kept seeing William's face when she told him no. And yet, if she hadn't. Gift of fate.

William lived in Palm Springs. That's all she knew. His cell phone number was on the nightstand. If she didn't catch him, she would stop, call Hidden Springs, ask them to find it for her.

I cannot have you give up a future for me, she would say. But it didn't have to be one or the other. Stupid to sabotage the now with the maybe. And she didn't care if it was two weeks or two months or two years. It didn't have to be forever. She knew what forever felt like.

Julia tapped the horn and a truck pulled over.

What was that book, that ridiculous book? Iowa housewife and photographer. Clint Eastwood and Meryl Streep in the movie. Bridges something. Stupid ending! How she hated that ending. Build this incredible off-the-chart, once-in-a-lifetime love, then pull the rug out. As if they wouldn't just wait until her kids were grown, then be together.

Ahead was the freeway, the overpass. She did not slow. The wheels lifted when she reached the top. God, airborne, a few feet. A squeal rose in her chest. Nice landing. Then flat, straight road all the way to Palm Springs, open desert on both sides. More cars, Monday morning traffic. She had expected to spot his truck in the distance.

So, all right, love always changes. Was that any reason not to find out? What was it William had said? "We simply do what we must. What we can't not do." And if it didn't work out, she had the world to taste now, real life, not just books. William's new plans didn't have to start tomorrow. It was summer. Mexico. Rosarito Beach. What was that like? Overlooking two coves, he'd said. The Pacific Ocean. She'd never seen the Pacific Ocean, except from the plane. Maybe they'd drive all the way to Cabo San Lucas. Hell, all the way to the tip of South America! Cape Horn. The Straits of Magellan. Rio.

And there were universities in Mexico. Guadalajara. They could learn Spanish together.

The morning sun glinted on the mountain to her right and she looked up. White rocks in that strange formation. She smiled. Tahquitz, the rascal god. Stealer of chickens. And women.

She looked again at the road, eyes blinded for a second. There, was that it? Or just a vision, heat mirages on asphalt?

No, not a mirage. She pushed the accelerator farther,

and then she realized. The truck up ahead was on the other side, coming toward her. William's Tacoma.

Easy, she thought. Gentle on the brake. No spinning out of control now.

They stopped on either side of the pavement, waited for an SUV to pass, then walked to the middle. A car they hadn't noticed honked, swerved past, the driver glaring out the window; what, are you fucking crazy?

Standing there in the middle of the road, grinning like fools.

"William," Julia said, "I have just one question."

"Anything," he said.

"Well . . ." She waited as a line of cars sped past.

William looked at her. Hair still tousled from their night, mascara smudges, little laugh lines showing in the morning sun. Beautiful. He drew her close, tried to shelter her from the wind whipped by the cars. Julia deserved better; even if it wasn't him, she deserved better. He had to tell her that.

The air quieted again after the last car.

He tilted her chin up. "You were saying?"

"What? Oh." Smiling, she pulled back, impossible to think with her head against his chest.

"Yes, well, I just want to know one thing."

Her voice mock serious, but not her eyes.

"This place in Rosarito Beach," she said. "Does it have dancing?"

"Does it have dancing!" He laughed as they hurried across. "Wait 'til you see." They stood by the Lamborghini's open bat door. "And . . . you think maybe I should know your real name?" he said.

"No," she teased, "not particularly. I never liked it, and I don't know yours."

"Javier." He did a slight bow. "Javier Dosamantes."

She studied him. "Javier. Oh, yes, that fits you much better." It was real. They were making it real.

He held out his hand, did his Sean Connery voice. "Well, it is my deepest pleasure to meet you, Miss . . ." He waited, watched her eyes, happy eyes, holding her secrets. What an adventure . . . like following a hummingbird. She didn't answer.

He let his hand drop. "Or, it doesn't matter. You can stay Julia."

"Yes," she said, "I think I will. Definitely." Firm, her business transaction voice.

And then she smiled, and he felt his cells renew.

"But just so you know," she said, "my name is, was . . . Evangeline. Eve."

HOT WATER

Readers Guide

1. Is it more intriguing to imagine a woman hiring a man for a weekend than the more typical *Pretty Woman* scenario? Why or why not? If it's only about sex, why is "Julia's" plan so empowering?

2. Throughout the novel we get glimpses into "Julia's" life at home. What is wrong with her marriage?

3. When do we start to know that "William" is not the stereotypical male escort?

4. Near the end of Chapter 11 there is a line: *He knew then precisely what she needed.* What does he mean? What does this tell us about "William" and about "Julia"?

5. Hidden Springs with its magic water and the Lamborghini Murcielago seem to be more than just a place/object. What does each contribute to "Julia's" adventure?

6. What function do Helen and Charles Wainwright have in the story?

7. What about "William's" other clients? Beyond the humor, what do these episodes show about some women's lives? And about "William"?

8. What does the novel have to say about our spiritual connection with nature?

9. How important is it that "William" is a philosophy major? Discuss the deeper levels in *Hot Water*, i.e., "Julia's" meditations on sin, their discussions of evil and the transcendence of love (Chapters 39–40). What does "the world has been broken for a long, long time" (Chapter 49–50) have to do with hot sex?

10. Is "William" representative of a shift in society as to how men and women see their roles? What are the ramifications of such a shift?

11. How do "William" and "Julia" change through the story? What is the significance in only revealing their real names at the end?

12. Women who break certain rules almost always get punished (e.g., Thelma and Louise, Marilyn Monroe). Yet "Julia," through cunning and "a gift of fate," not only escapes punishment but is rewarded beyond her wildest dreams. At least so far. Is this only a fantasy? Will they live happily ever after? Does it matter?